A Candlelight Regency Special

D0833287

CANDLELIGHT REGENCIES

THE IMPOVERISHED HEIRESS

Diana Burke

A CANDLELIGHT REGENCY SPECIAL

Published by
Dell Publishing Co., Inc.
1 Dag Hammarskjold Plaza
New York, New York 10017

Dell ® TM 681510, Dell Publishing Co., Inc.

ISBN: 0-440-13842-6

Printed in the United States of America
First printing—October 1981

THE
IMPOVERISHED
HEIRESS

CHAPTER 1

A muffled shriek from the large drawing room brought Miss Samantha Crawford to a pause at the foot of the stairs. Suppressing an exclamation of annoyance, she crossed the parquet floor of the hall and threw open the double doors. Then, fixing the occupants with a stern glance, she asked for an explanation.

"Please, miss, 'twas my fault," admitted the young footman who was perched atop a ladder in the middle of the long room. From that precarious position, he gave her a jerky bow.

Miss Crawford's expression relented at that comic display, and she forced back a smile of amusement. Both underservants were new and as yet untrained, but they did show signs of promise, Samantha realized. The room was nearly ready to receive guests. The Holland covers had been removed, and the floor, the windows, and the highly polished mahogany furniture shone cleanly in the afternoon sun.

Robert rushed on with his explanation. "Jenny was handing me up the clean prisms, and I dropped one."

"'Tisn't broke, miss. Truly," Jenny promised, her face scarlet with embarrassment. "It fell on the carpet and didn't even crack. I'm sorry I yelled, miss."

"Never mind then. Just get on with your work. Robert, as soon as you've removed the ladder, fetch the flowers from the scullery. I've finished arranging them. But hurry, both of you. The family will be arriving within the hour."

How to prepare for so many guests when half the house had been closed up for years was causing some anxiety. With only a fortnight's notice the small staff had been hard put to manage. Nevertheless the stately Palladian mansion was being put to rights again.

Furnished elegantly in what was the height of fashion thirty years before and never altered since, it had been condemned as "horrid bare and plain" by no less an authority than Miss Crawford's cousin, Amelia Dakins. Yet to Samantha's eyes the delicate Hepplewhite furniture and the nobly proportioned rooms of her grandfather's house were beautiful. An infrequent visitor at her cousin's home on the other side of the nearby village of Little Ditchling, Samantha never could admire the ornate Empire-style trappings that fashionably cluttered Dakins Hall, although affection for her own home did not blind her to its defects.

Despite all her care there was still much amiss at the Pillars. There had been nothing she could do about the sun-rotted drapes in the drawing room, or the ragged tear in the dining room carpet where Bess, Grandfather's favorite bitch, had been wont to take her bones, nor all the other places where only ready cash could solve the problem. And that had been woefully scarce for too long. Would the new heir understand that the shabbiness so apparent to a discerning eye was not her fault? Grandfather had turned miserly in his old age, grudging every penny, and since the Crawford fortune was reckoned to be enormous, his tightfistedness was hard to forgive.

In a determined rush Miss Crawford mounted the stairs, for she still needed to inspect the guest rooms. The heir had been allotted Grandfather's room, as it was by far in the best condition. Would it shake him that the old man had died in it a bare three months before? Of course, a soldier would have no foolish sensibility to overcome, unlike Samantha, who had to steel herself each time it was necessary to enter that somber room. The huge oak bedstead brought over from the old Crawford manor when the Pillars was built still seemed mysteriously filled with Phineas's commanding and irascible presence.

After checking that the bedding was fresh and well aired, and that there were clean towels and soap by the washstand, Samantha lingered irresolutely in the doorway. She remembered kneeling by the bed as the old man lay dying. He'd roused just once after the stroke that had brought him down, and even then Samantha could see no sign of affection in the restless glance he bestowed on her.

"Grandfather?" she whispered hopefully, her hand groping for his on the coverlet.

"The land has to go to a Crawford," he had said clearly, "to carry on the name."

"I understand." Samantha consoled him.

9

"I did my best for you," he muttered. Then added querulously, "Should have been a boy. That's the trouble." He said no more after that but stared at the ceiling and shortly lapsed into unconsciousness.

It was a very unsatisfactory sort of leave-taking. To the last he refused to acknowledge the comfort his granddaughter had brought to him over the years, nor did he even accord her a thank you for the loving attention that had made his last days so peaceful.

But Samantha had no time for useless regrets. Continuing her progress down the long corridor, she peeped into the room that was to be Mrs. Dakins's and found all prepared, even to the bowl of chrysanthemums on the dressing table. It was a charming room, and Aunt Anne would have nothing of which to complain, or so Samantha hoped.

On down the hall were smaller bedrooms, one each for her cousins: Jasper, Amelia, and Elizabeth. Everything was in order there. The room at the end of the corridor she had saved for Mr. Ponsoby, the lawyer down from London. It was not as fine as the others, but short of putting him in the green room again, there was nothing else for it. On his last visit he had complained about the royal bedroom allotted him, saying that its mammoth proportions were too awesome for a man of his dimensions. True, the oversized bed did tend to dwarf the rather slight Londoner, but at the time it was the only guest room not in a complete state of disorder. Even now all bedrooms in the east wing of the house were closed for lack of enough linens.

If all at the Pillars was not as it should be, it was

partly Mr. Ponsoby's fault anyway. He'd been unconscionably tight with the purse strings since Grandfather's death in June, sending her barely enough money to run the house. There were debts outstanding everywhere, especially in the village. Most worrying was the bill from the wine merchant demanding immediate payment. The Crawford farms too were dreadfully neglected, and poor Huddle's cottage was nearly roofless. Samantha had promised to help the tenants with her own inheritance. But the bills . . . was she or the new heir to the estate responsible for them?

At least, by this time tomorrow, the will would have been read, and she'd be free from these disquieting anxieties. Having to wait all summer for Major Wyndham Crawford to return from the Continent after Bonaparte's defeat was wearing on the nerves. Mr. Ponsoby insisted that the new heir be present for the reading of the will, and while that was very correct of him, it only made Samantha more impatient to free the estate from these embarrassing debts.

It was particularly galling because there had to be plenty of money stashed away in some London bank vault. Grandfather's attitude had been "Let 'em wait," and wait they had. It was little wonder that the tradesmen had grown impatient. Samantha decided long ago that when she inherited the fortune her grandfather had promised her, things would be different. What good was money locked up in a strongbox? Yet it was not so much what the money could buy that Samantha coveted, as the freedom that her fortune would allow her, a freedom denied her by her demanding grandsire.

She tried hard not to blame the old man for his indifference. Phineas Crawford was never reconciled to the loss of his own two headstrong, quarrelsome boys. The elder, Robert, had died in '97 in the war with France, while Samantha's father, Charles, was never forgiven for joining the diplomatic corps and dying abroad. That Phineas's only grandchild was a pale, quiet girl seemed to him a bitter joke, and he treated her with selfish disregard.

Samantha's only link with her parents now was nanny Bunch, once her mother's nurse and then her own. Now as she slipped thankfully into the haven of her own room, Bunch's scolding voice met her.

"Where have you been, my lambie? Working yourself to death, I'll be bound. How will you look your best to greet those fine ladies and gentlemen when you've left yourself no time to dress?"

"Don't fuss at me, Bunch. You know I must see that everything is in readiness. Cook was in such a taking at the thought of four courses and seven to sit down to dinner tonight!"

"I suppose I must be grateful you haven't took it into your head to help out down there. Seven! As if that were anything! Why, I remember when this house has held twenty for a week, and all their abigails and valets belowstairs, besides."

"Then you remember more than I do. All I can recollect is Mr. Ponsoby who always came to bother Grandfather about business. I don't count the Dakinses."

Nanny Bunch sniffed her disapproval of the Dakinses as she slipped off Samantha's lilac-colored muslin dress and began to brush out her silver-gilt hair. It was long and thick and so blond as to appear almost white. Samantha gazed at it with disfavor. "How dull it looks."

"Now why should you be sayin' a thing like that? It's lovely hair, the same as your mother's. What you need is a proper lady's maid. With the rheumatics in my hands so bad, I can't do much but brush it and knot it up for you. It needs to be cut and curled."

"I don't want or need anyone but you, Bunch," Samantha said decidedly with an affectionate look at her old nurse. "And pray, why should I try to make my hair beautiful?" she continued, casting a cynical smile at her own reflection.

"If you don't know by now, there's not a bit of use in me telling you," snapped back the old woman as she stuck in the last comb.

"You are an incurable romantic, to be dreaming dreams at your age! Oh, I know you'd like to see me wed to this Wyndham Crawford, but he's probably old, a terrible rake, and ugly to boot!"

"He's the heir, missy—and no fool, or he wouldn't have served on Wellington's staff, neither." Like everyone else in England after Waterloo, Bunch tended to hero-worship the Iron Duke.

"Well, our curiosity will be appeased this afternoon. How silly Grandfather was! Wouldn't have the man in his house because of some family quarrel, and yet felt he must leave him the entire estate in his will."

Samantha spoke dispassionately as Bunch slipped her best dress of black sarcenet over her head and adjusted the ruffles of fine lawn that adorned neck and wrists. Unrelieved black was not flattering to Samantha, but it was dictated by the custom of mourning. With her hair strained back from her face and the severely simple gown, her delicate coloring was reduced to an insipid pallor. Though her features were good, an aquiline nose and a wide mouth gave her more character than was generally allowed to be pretty. Still, her gentian-blue eyes, wide, candid, and intelligent, redeemed the too angular face from plainness.

Bunch looked dourly in the glass, noting and resenting for her mistress the signs of strain and overwork in the too pale cheeks, the almost bone-thin shoulders. "Happen the old man had his reasons, though I'll not speak ill of the dead by telling 'em."

"Never mind, Bunch. Major Crawford can have the Pillars for all I care! We'll have our own little house and enough money to travel, as well. How would you like to see France?"

"Oh, I could stand it, I guess," the old woman spoke grudgingly, but there was a smile lurking in her eyes. Poor lambie! Little enough joy had come her way. Now with her inheritance and shed of this big old barn of a place, she'd have a chance for happiness, at last. Wicked old woman that she was, she'd prayed for the old man to die. Even so, the old miser had hung on too long, keeping Miss Samantha bound and tied to him. Here she was twenty-six and with no more knowledge of men or the world than a babe unborn. And it wouldn't hurt for her to get away, neither. Too worried about other folks' business was Miss Samantha. One day her being wishful to help was going to take her too far. Even Perkins, butler at the Pillars, and Bunch's greatest ally, was wont to fill Miss Samantha's head with all sorts of notions, like she was responsible for the welfare of those good-for-nothing tenants. If they wanted to court danger by smuggling, that was their problem, and not one for Miss Sam to concern herself with.

"How do I look, Bunch?"

The unaccustomed question shook the old nurse from her thoughts. It was not like Miss Samantha to worry about her appearance nor need reassurances, either. "You look beautiful as always, missy," she answered fondly.

The sound of carriage wheels on gravel sent Samantha hurrying to the door, flustered a little to think of welcoming her guests. She paused to blow a kiss back through the doorway to the one person in the world who loved her unreservedly. Then, forcing herself to a calm and graceful pace, she descended the paneled staircase, gazed on by the painted eyes of long-dead Crawfords. Her black kid slippers were soundless on the steps, and she was unobserved as she approached the hall where the Dakins family was busily making its presence felt.

"If you'll wait in here, please." Perkins was ushering the ladies into the drawing room, but Jasper had caught sight of his cousin standing on the landing above. Putting a finger to his lips, he hushed the words of welcome she had almost spoken.

Swiftly ascending the stairs, he lifted Samantha's hand to his lips. "Sweet Coz, our reward is almost due."

Samantha pulled away from Jasper's warm clasp and smoothed her dress. "Jasper, really," she reproved.

"Can't help it. Mama's been in a fret to hear what the old man left us. Not much, I reckon, as we ain't Crawfords." And he waved his hand airily as if to indicate that his words weren't as avaricious as they sounded. "You're looking deuced tired, Sammie. Thought once the old boy popped off, you'd perk up and smile. Still pretty, of course," he added hastily.

Samantha smiled in exasperation. Of all her cousins Jasper was her favorite. A scapegrace boy, spoiled by his widowed mother and two sisters, Jasper counted heavily on his darkly handsome face to excuse him from all his frequent sins. Naturally it hadn't helped him much with old Phineas, who never did more than endure the Dakins brood, although they were his wife's brother's children. Still, unlike his nearer kin, they managed to stay on tolerably good terms with the old man, and Jasper had ridden over to pay a call on his cousin and the tightfisted master of the Pillars quite often.

Perhaps now his devotion was about to pay off in a pleasant little bequest. And since Jasper was passionately addicted to horses and horse racing, the money would be welcome despite his pretense to the contrary.

Perkins cleared his throat, and Samantha looked

16

pointedly at the booted foot that barred her progress. "Shall we join your mama?" she asked.

"S'pose we must," Jasper replied glumly and dutifully offered Samantha his arm.

Mrs. Dakins had read him a lecture on the way over, telling him to waste no time in fixing Samantha's regard. She was sure to inherit a goodly share of the gold that was reportedly stacked in the cellars of the Pillars, and marrying her would be a painless way to enjoy its benefits. But it was difficult to play the lover with Samantha when she still treated him as if he were a recalcitrant ten-year-old, for all he was six months older than she.

Perkins opened the double doors and bowed them through. The butler was old and apprehensive of the changes to come. Perhaps the new heir would find his services *de trop*. He, more than Samantha, was aware of how things had slipped from the standards of a gentleman's country home in the last years. The new master was sure to find much to fault in the staff, a staff that was either too old or rawly young.

As he hurried downstairs to fetch the Madeira for the guests, he hoped his failing hearing would warn him in time if the Major should arrive in the interval.

In the drawing room Jasper's mama was refusing all refreshment. A wisp of a woman who affected an air of fragility belied by the steel of her will, Anne Dakins sighed heavily as she put one hand to her head. "No, dear Samantha, I couldn't touch a thing. I must just go lie down. Perhaps I'll be recovered by dinner. Amelia, Elizabeth, you must come up and rest, too."

Elizabeth rose with obedient alacrity, but Amelia turned a stubborn face to her mother and said she wasn't a bit tired, no indeed. There was a brief battle of wills in the locked glances of mother and daughter, and for once, the mother yielded.

"Come along, Elizabeth," she said, throwing Jasper a meaningful glance as she stood up, but Samantha avoided the trap with accustomed skill, insisting sweetly that she must show her guests to their rooms.

Mrs. Dakins gave her bedroom a critical appraisal and asked how long before her trunk would be brought up. Samantha promised that it and the lady's maid, a new role for Jenny, would arrive shortly, then excused herself and went to see to Elizabeth.

Elizabeth, just out of the schoolroom at seventeen, was delighted with her own small quarters and thanked Samantha nicely for the posy of flowers by the bed. "Mother said you are to come to London with us this season. I'll be coming out, and you will be, as well," she prattled happily.

"Dear Elizabeth! I am much too old to come out. Why it is at least eight years too late to be thinking of it."

"Well, not 'come out' exactly," Elizabeth stuttered, pleating and unpleating the blue satin ribbon that was threaded under the bust of her white muslin gown. "But you could go to some concerts and be presented at court and buy some new clothes . . . Why, Mama says you would be quite a success if you let her guide you!"

Samantha felt a pang at that. Why hadn't Mrs. Dakins offered such an invitation years before when

18

Samantha was almost dying from ennui and the stifled dreams of youth? The reason, of course, was that Grandfather would have nipped any such scheme in the bud, perhaps had for all she knew. Not that he denied her the fundamental instructions to take her bow in polite society, just the opportunity to show off her accomplishments. At eighteen, when Samantha should have been presented, Phineas arbitrarily decided it was not necessary. Samantha tried explaining that to Elizabeth now.

"I might go down with the Crawford money as a sweetener. But no, Elizabeth. I've decided to retire to a small house in Brighton and live very quietly with nanny Bunch. I've been at the beck and call of Grandfather so long I'm not anxious to trade my independence away for any husband, be he ever so charming."

Elizabeth was shocked, for she devoutly believed that a woman's only hope of happiness was as a wife and mother. The fact that the reverse was very often the case had escaped her notice.

"Surely you're joking, Cousin?" she asked, her pansy-brown eyes dilated in consternation.

Samantha shook her head, but before she could startle her gentle visitor again with her iconoclastic ideas, there came a hurried knock on the door.

"Miss, oh, miss! The heir! He's come, and Perkins don't know what to do. He's shown him into the drawing room. Oh, come down, miss, please!"

Samantha frowned at the maid's agitation and hushed her sternly. "That will do, Jenny. Tell Perkins I'll be there directly." Then she turned back to

Elizabeth. "I'll see you at six in the dining room. Rest well, dear."

Elizabeth smiled a nervous assent. Cousin Samantha was a little intimidating with her air of calm authority. She was old, of course, but Elizabeth envied her her *sang-froid*. Little did she guess with what trepidation Samantha was approaching the drawing room door.

Perkins hovered in the hall, looking distressed.

"Yes, Perkins?" Samantha's voice was cool and steady.

"Forgive me, miss. I shouldn't have put the Major in the drawing room to wait. I didn't hear him at first and then, well, I forgot that Mr. Dakins and Miss Amelia were in there."

"Oh, I'm sure it will be all right. A little awkward that the guests had to introduce themselves, but I think we can assume that the Major has survived worse ordeals."

"Yes, miss."

"Just come in with me and serve everyone a little wine. Courage, Perkins!"

At that, a tremulous smile lighted up the old butler's face, and he squared his shoulders. Opening the doors, he announced in beautifully rounded tones, "Miss Samantha Crawford."

CHAPTER 2

Major Wyndham Crawford arrived at the Pillars in the glow of a fine September afternoon. The drive from London to England's southern coast had been pleasant but tiring. Although he had stopped at Worthing for lunch, an excellent repast in a waterfront inn where one did not question the excise stamp on the innkeeper's brandy, he was anxious to see the end of his journey.

Pulling up in the graveled drive beside the imposing colonnade that gave the house its name, he could see no evidence of life. The rows of windows, each with an eyebrow of stone facing, looked sightlessly back at him.

The Major handed the reins of his restive team of bays to his tiger. "Take them around back, Jem, and see that they are properly housed. Then send someone in with my trunks."

Jem touched his cap and led the matched pair around the side of the house, promising himself a rare time dressing down whatever worthless sort of stable lads were to be found here. They must be both deaf and dumb to ignore the master's arrival.

Climbing the short flight of stairs to the front door, the Major rapped sharply on it with the butt of his whip. After a considerable delay the door was opened by an elderly butler, his dignity somewhat impaired by his being out of breath.

"Major Crawford?" he wheezed. "I'm Perkins, sir. If you'll step this way, I'll tell Miss Crawford that you're here."

Wyndham Crawford found himself in a long, pleasant room, where he was relieved of hat and whip before he realized that he was not alone. Two young people were staring at him. One was a very pretty girl dressed in the latest mode, her hair a mass of black ringlets and her green eyes bright with interest. The other, evidently her brother, for the family resemblance was strong, was a dandified youth who wore an enormous and intricately tied cravat. Frowning at being so suddenly thrust among strangers, the Major stared back. "Who are you?" he asked brusquely.

The young girl curtsied, dimpling into a coquettish smile. "We have the advantage of knowing who you must be. Major Wyndham Crawford, hero of the Peninsular Campaign and heir apparent to all this."

"Be quiet, Amelia," her brother hissed, attempting unsuccessfully to frown her down. "I'm Jasper Dakins, and this is my sister, Amelia. Phineas Crawford was our great-uncle. By marriage, I hasten to add. In the absence of Miss Crawford, we welcome you to the Pillars."

The young man's attitude was too playful and informal to please the Major. He returned the bow formally. "Thank you, Mr. Dakins, Miss Dakins. I am, as you surmised, Wyndham Crawford, but I make no claim to the title of hero."

"Oh," Amelia cried in mock dismay, glancing up at him through delightfully curly lashes. "And I thought my source of information reliable!"

The Major rather thawed at that. "You'll have to judge for yourself, miss."

She gave him a saucy smile at this invitation. "Be sure I will!" she exclaimed.

The newcomer was looking around the room rather thoughtfully. It was not what he had expected. The salon had an air of faded splendor, for the sunlight streaming in through the windows cruelly revealed the shabbiness of rubbed-thin upholstery on the gilt chairs, of velvet drapes that hung in tatters from the lofty ceiling.

Jasper and Amelia were busy taking in the Major's appearance. He was dressed very quietly in a coat of blue superfine, while his cravat, unlike Jasper's, made no attempt at the elaboration of fashion. His cool gray eyes, a strongly determined chin, and the reddish-brown hair that curled attractively over his fine forehead were pleasing enough, but it was the white scar that ran diagonally from cheek to eyebrow that held their attention. The saber cut gave him a dangerous air that was accentuated by his military bearing and the rather hard expression of his mouth.

The door opened just then, and Jasper stepped forward with relief. "Samantha, may I present Major Wyndham Crawford."

The Major bowed stiffly, hiding his surprise with

difficulty. This tall, slender woman was dressed in so modest a style, he would have taken her for Miss Crawford's companion rather than Phineas's granddaughter.

Samantha too was surprised. The reality of Major Wyndham Crawford was far closer to Bunch's expectations than her own. He was neither old nor ugly, but almost handsome if it weren't for that unfortunate scar on his face. The Major looked to be no more than thirty-five.

Samantha smiled. "It is very pleasant to discover another member of my family. I've always felt deprived that I had only Grandfather."

"And us," Jasper added jealously. "You've always had us."

The Major looked his disapproval at Jasper's vehemence, and Samantha was stirred to a warmer reply than was perhaps warranted.

"Of course, dear Cousin. That goes without saying."

The young man so addressed received her smile with a smug expression that was not lost on the Major, and if he leaped to the logical conclusion that Miss Crawford and Mr. Dakins had an understanding, he was not so much wrong, perhaps, as misdirected.

The party in the drawing room soon broke up only to reassemble some two hours later, augmented by the presence of Mr. Ponsoby, who had arrived shortly before by mail coach from London. They gathered in the blue salon again where the fire crackling on the hearth and the once opulent blue damask chairs made an appropriate setting for the rustling silk of the ladies' gowns and the formality of the gentlemen's evening clothes.

The glow from the fire mingled with the last of the daylight to soften and beautify the room, and even Mr. Ponsoby, whose dried-up face seemed incapable of expressing anything but a lawyerlike caution, was almost human as he chatted in the corner with Mrs. Dakins. Anne would have been most happy to discover exactly what portion of Phineas's considerable fortune was to come to her family, but her charming efforts were to no avail, for even firelight and smiling eyes could not tempt Mr. Ponsoby into an indiscretion.

Though everyone was equally interested in tomorrow's business, the subject of the will was for the most part avoided. A vulgar curiosity may have troubled many a heart, but it was kept in check. All were united in one assumption; Miss Crawford would be amply repaid for her years of devotion to her grandfather, even though the house and land were destined to go to the male heir.

Amelia, with the practice of two London Seasons behind her, was flirting with the Major. "Please," she begged prettily, "tell me about Wellington. Is he really very stern? He must be awe-inspiring, the genius who outwitted Boney."

"Yes, he is a great man, but not stern. At least, not with the ladies, whom he greatly admires." The Major smiled agreeably into Miss Dakins's eyes. He was feeling happy. And why not? The war was over, and he had managed to come out of it in one piece, which was more than he could say for a lot of poor devils. Furthermore he was about to inherit a very fine property. A little neglected to be sure, but he could handle that. The Major rather relished the challenge.

Samantha had determined that much about him already by his air of command. His military manner of address was forceful, to say the least. Yet it did not escape her notice how he softened perceptively when speaking to Amelia.

Jasper caught one of the interested glances Samantha bestowed on the Major, and he immediately began coaxing her to take a stroll on the terrace.

"But it's dark and cold," she protested.

"Nonsense. We need a breath of fresh air. Besides, there's still a bit of sunset, or there was a moment ago."

Perhaps Samantha, as the Major, was happy at the thought of tomorrow's promise, for she finally consented to being led out the French doors onto the twilit terrace. Shivering slightly, she gazed at the slivered moon that hung in the sky as the last fingers of gold on the horizon faded into gloom.

"Dear Samantha, I must ask you . . ."

"Oh, no, Jasper," Samantha was annoyed. "Not again. I thought we had resolved that. We should not suit, whatever your mama thinks. This is too bad of you. You promised!"

"But why won't you marry me? We could be happy. There's not another girl I'd rather spend my life with . . . and that's the truth, Sammie!" Jasper had captured both her hands and was smiling coaxingly.

26

"The truth is, I know you too well, Jasper," Samantha laughed. "You'd be forever getting into scrapes and expecting me to bail you out. No. No thank you, indeed. And if you try this again, I shall be really angry!"

"If you won't, you won't," Jasper spoke philosophically. "But we're still friends, aren't we?"

Samantha sighed. The Dakins's had been the only family on intimate terms at the Pillars and despite their shortcomings, their companionship had redeemed many a lonely day for her. She shook his hand. "Still friends, Jasper."

They strolled to the far end of the terrace and looked out over the dark lawn to where the avenue of lime trees stood silhouetted against the sky.

"You know how I've always wanted to breed horses, Sammie? Good lines. I could do it, too. I've a chance to buy into a partnership in Ireland."

"Buy a partnership? With what?"

Jasper looked reproachful. "You don't give me much credit, do you, Sam?"

"I'm sorry, Jasper. It's just that you're such a dreamer."

"It's not a dream this time. It could be a very good business proposition. But of course, you're right. I need capital to buy in. A lot. If there's a nice little bequest for me, I'll be fine. Otherwise . . ." He sighed despondently.

Samantha knew very well that the chances of her grandfather's leaving anything to the Dakinses were remote indeed. "Oh, dear," she murmured.

"You know, don't you? There isn't. It's been quite an evening, Sam."

"Don't sound so bleak. There's always a way if you really want it enough to work for it."

"You mean a miracle? 'Fraid I don't believe in them."

"Perhaps I might . . ."

"Help? Oh, Sammie! If you only would! I'd pay you back in no time."

Taken aback by Jasper's hasty assumption, Samantha said uneasily. "Well, I suppose I could . . ."

"Oh, Coz, thank you! You'll never regret it. I'll make us both rich." And he kissed her hands in a passion of gratitude.

While it was very pleasant to play Lady Bountiful, Samantha was doubtful that Mr. Ponsoby would give his consent quite so readily. There might be strings attached to her inheritance. And those debts . . . she still might have to pay them.

"Let's go in," she said hastily, suddenly cold in the night air.

They turned to see Major Crawford just about to reenter the house also. How long had he been on the terrace, and what had he heard of their conversation? There was a conscious look on his face that seemed to indicate it was quite a lot.

CHAPTER 3

Major Wyndham Crawford had risen early.
Whether it was from sleeping in a strange bed or the
exhilaration that comes with all beginnings, he found
himself awake at dawn. It was rather like going into
battle, he reflected with a wry grin. By seven he was
dressed and heading for the stables, only to be way-
laid by Perkins on the stair.

"Good morning, sir. Breakfast is in the little dining room at nine, but if you would like some coffee,
I could bring you some immediately—and perhaps a
scone or two."

"Thank you, Perkins. That sounds excellent."

"In here, sir." Tactfully Perkins steered the Major
into the morning room.

"It will take me awhile to learn my way around,
I'm afraid."

"You'll soon have the hang of it, sir. The Pillars
is quite a convenient house. The master planned it
himself, and you'll find that it's laid out very rationally. Not like the old manor with its long draughty
passages and secret stairs, and the kitchen miles from

anywhere. You'll soon feel at home, sir. I'll send the maid in to prepare the fire."

Left alone, Major Crawford occupied himself by examining the chamber. It was an oddity, done in the *chinoiserie* that had captivated tastes many years before. A faded red Turkey carpet covered much of the polished wood floor, and several Chippendale armchairs, their seats upholstered with an oriental silk, were scattered about. A large serpentine-fronted sideboard stood against one wall, while two small japanned tables were arranged near the windows. The brocade draperies were at one time as colorful as the red-roofed pagodas and fire-breathing dragons that writhed on the wallpaper, but sun and time had bleached their crimson to a dull rose. Even so, the room had a quaint charm that Wyndham found appealing.

His inspection was interrupted by a timid knock at the door which opened to admit a young maid, her arms filled with wood for the small tiled fireplace in the corner. Overcome at finding the new heir standing in the middle of the room when she expected Miss Samantha to be waiting, Jenny took one frightened look at his scarred face and let out an undignified screech before sending her armload of kindling scattering in all directions.

"What nonsense is this?" he barked at her. "Am I a monster to frighten the maids now?"

"Sorry, sir." Jenny was red with mortification as she bent over to pick up the wood.

"Well, get the fire started, girl. No need to snivel either. I won't eat you."

30

When Miss Crawford entered the room a few minutes later, she found Jenny busily brushing bits of wood and bark off the sleeves of the Major's coat.

"Good morning," Samantha greeted him in polite surprise. "What happened to you?"

The Major seemed embarrassed. "Nothing calamitous. But your servants need drilling, ma'am," he grumbled.

Samantha stiffened at that and shot an inquiring glance at Jenny. But the little maid only ducked her head in a quick curtsy and scuttled out of the room, too shy to thank the Major for his assistance.

"Jenny is still young and untrained, but I think she will prove to be an excellent servant in time. How did she muss your coat?"

"Never mind. Will you join me for coffee? Perkins is bringing some."

"No, thank you. I've a great deal to do this morning."

"I'm sure you'll manage all the better after a light repast," and he led her firmly over to the table. "Oh, there you are, Perkins. Fetch another cup for Miss Crawford, won't you?"

Perkins was almost smug. "There's service for two here, Major. I thought perhaps Miss Samantha would join you as she is customarily an early riser."

The tea trolly Perkins had rolled into the room was heavily laden. There were eggs, sausages, kippered herrings, and paper-thin slices of bread and butter as well as the promised scones and honey— not to mention a silver pot from which wafted the heavenly scent of freshly brewed coffee. "There is China tea if you prefer, miss."

The Major was eyeing the array of dishes with a sardonic smile. "I suppose this isn't breakfast?"

"No, sir," Perkins replied seriously. "Breakfast will be served at nine, but Cook thought you might like a bite before you ride out."

"Thank Cook and tell her she needn't bother about breakfast, at least for me. This will do quite nicely."

"Yes, sir."

The closing door brought Samantha to life. "I really must go see to the household," she said, trying to sound firm.

"Sit down and have something to eat. Tea or coffee? Do you take cream?"

Unaccountably Samantha found herself allowing the Major to present her with a plate piled high with some of everything. "I never eat in the mornings," she protested.

"Then you should. It's much healthier." He sat down at the opposite side of the table. "Are you always up and about before breakfast," he asked shrewdly, "or are your guests particularly troublesome this morning?"

Samantha was uncomfortably aware of his critical examination. "I am quite able to deal with my guests, Major. That has been one of my responsibilities for many years now, especially since my grandfather's health began to fail."

"Oh? Was there something wrong with him besides old age and meanness? I didn't know."

Samantha looked up, shocked, not sure if he were serious or not. "You aren't very respectful of the dead," she countered unsmilingly.

"*De mortuis nil nisi bonum?* Seems to me there are very few tears being shed for old Phineas. Even you must be planning how to spend your inheritance, if you don't give it away first."

Samantha flushed at that reminder of last night's events. Major Crawford had evidently heard enough to decide that Jasper has gulled her into a foolish concession. Lifting her chin, she met his gray eyes candidly. "Heiresses can afford to be magnanimous."

"Unquestionably, Miss Crawford."

Watching the play of emotion on her face, the Major marveled at how little disguise those blue eyes had. Only moments before they had revealed a lively embarrassment, while now they expressed only cold disapproval. His criticism of Phineas had been resented. He had not been tactful, he admitted to himself. Intrigued by the signs of intelligence and spirit he recognized in her, he wondered that she could be content to marry her cousin, Jasper Dakins. Yet Mrs. Dakins had assured him that the young couple were to announce their engagement shortly.

The Major was used to sizing up men, and he had already decided that Jasper was a lightweight. When Wyndham stepped out on the terrace last night to smoke a cheroot, he had inadvertently overheard the fellow double-talk Miss Crawford into a large loan. Dakins must be desperate to risk queering his pitch before the wedding. Was the girl about to be saddled with a load of debts? A poor beginning for an inauspicious marriage.

Changing the subject, Samantha asked, "Were you planning to ride this morning? I hear you brought your own mount. That was wise of you. The stables are sadly depleted these days since Grandfather gave up hunting. However, MacNamara is a good man and will be delighted to see prime horseflesh again."

"Yes. I thought to ride out. I want to inspect the estate. Would you come with me? I confess I could use a guide."

Samantha hesitated before answering. Of all things, she loved an early morning gallop, although the aging Pegasus was no fit mount for anything past a canter these days. And perhaps she might tactfully show the Major the things that required his immediate attention. "I'd like to," she began, "but . . ." And a vision of all that needed doing rose up to reproach her.

"But?" he prompted.

"I should see that the breakfast trays are sent up, and I must talk to Cook about the menus. Oh, there are a hundred things! I'm afraid I can't come."

"Surely the housekeeper can attend to all that," he said impatiently.

"There isn't any housekeeper, or rather I am she."

"You? What? Old Phineas must have been all about in the head. It is utterly unsuitable for a young girl to have the burden . . ." As the Major noticed the offended expression on the lady's face, his strictures petered out. "Well, surely Perkins can manage this morning?"

34

"I'm afraid not." The Major's comments had nettled, but of course they were only what Bunch had been saying for years.

"I never knew the old gentleman, and now I must say I'm happy to have been spared the pleasure. Lady Fitzcameron was fairly pungent in her analysis of his character. And I supposed she was exaggerating!"

"Do you mean Grandfather's sister? Aunt Hester?"

"Have you met her?"

"Oh, no. But Grandfather mentioned her once or twice." The reserve of that statement clearly reflected what Phineas might have said about his strong-minded sister.

The Major smiled with amusement. "Lady Fitz and your grandfather were my father's second cousins, as you know, and I spent a few summer holidays on the Fitzcameron estate in Ireland after my father died. I wanted to follow in his footsteps and be a soldier also. Hester encouraged my youthful dream, and whenever on leave from my duties, her house in London was always open to me. She's a grand old girl, though no doubt as autocratic as your grandfather in her own way. It's a Crawford failing."

Samantha couldn't help but be intrigued by the topic of her Great-aunt Hester. She and Phineas had quarreled bitterly and irrevocably over his decision to abandon the old family manor house and erect the Pillars as a more fitting residence for a man of his wealth. Samantha had always admired Hester for standing up to her brother, although she herself never considered such a move. He had drummed it into her head that she owed him an obligation for taking her in and providing her with a home. The years she spent as housekeeper, nurse, and companion could scarcely repay the debt.

In her younger days Samantha had longed to leave the Pillars and take her place in society, but Phineas's insistence that she stay at home where she was needed had seen those dreams slowly fade. Now, at twenty-six, she was prepared to face the world practically. Romance was for other people, not for an aging spinster, no matter how wealthy.

"Grandfather was difficult," Samantha admitted, "but in his own way he was good to me. You see, he would have preferred a boy."

"So, for the most part he treated you like one, laying too many responsibilities on your shoulders. Did you never go to London?"

"No, but my cousins live nearby, and they do visit frequently."

The Major could imagine the dutiful weekends suffered by the Dakinses in hopes of currying favor with the old scoundrel. But according to Ponsoby, there was no mention of them in the will. The thought was thoroughly satisfying. "I gathered from the conversation last night that Miss Dakins doesn't care for the country."

Samantha missed the note of irony in his voice and answered sincerely. "That's true, but Amelia gets to Brighton and London often enough to keep her from fretting too much."

"Yet you don't accompany her? Why not?"

"Grandfather thought it would be a waste of time for me and truly, I must concur. I wouldn't shine at a ball."

He gave her an honest appraisal, then said frankly, "Why wouldn't you do as well as any other young lady? You look a little underfed, but there's nothing wrong with you, is there?"

Samantha was affronted at the man's bald rudeness. "That is not the point," she said repressively. "I prefer the quiet life of the country and do not wish to waste my time in the frivolous pursuits of society."

"Frivolous! How do you know? You haven't had a chance to see if you like it or not. Your grandfather was a scoundrel, Miss Crawford. What was he, some sort of Bible thumper? How were you to make a decent marriage stuck away in this house?" He looked at her critically. "If you'd eat properly and take that silly cap off your head, you'd be a fine-looking woman. And even if you were as ugly as sin, I suppose you could enjoy the theatre, the conversation, and the shopping as well as any woman. You'd best get yourself to London. I think you'll find a great deal to enjoy in the 'frivolous pursuits of society.' "

Samantha's hand strayed involuntarily to her frilled cap. Bunch had begged her not to wear it today. "This is a ridiculous conversation, Major."

"No doubt," he answered shortly, annoyed that he had been led into saying what had so clearly shocked and offended this poor little mouse of a cousin. When would he learn to curb his wretched tongue?

Samantha rose, leaving her scarcely touched plate. "I must go. Enjoy your ride, Major."

Despite a firm decision to forget it, Samantha found her thoughts returning to this surprising breakfast conversation. The Major was certainly outspoken, too much so, a fault not checked in his years of military service. Underfed, indeed! Still, he was right about one thing. She knew too little of the world of society to condemn it. The thought of the theatre, of concerts, of small parties where witty conversation and mild flirtations enlivened the evening was terribly enticing. But it was probably too late now. She could never enter society as the artless debutantes did, on a wave of parties and dance music. Society for a spinster lady of indeterminate years would hold few of the delights that the Major had described. Besides there was no one to introduce her, to take her around. Even all the Crawford money would be no help. It would attract tricksters and confidence men, as her grandfather had warned her over and over. Samantha shrank from the idea of being gulled by some plausible fortune hunter. No. A small house in Brighton seemed infinitely preferable to the dangers of London. Independence, not social triumph, was her goal, after all. And with her inheritance it was in sight, at last: some new clothes, the leisure to travel, and the comforting presence of Bunch. Surely those modest desires could be fulfilled?

The Major's inheritance was more problematic, for with the Pillars he had received a difficult, even onerous task. He might decide that reclaiming a rundown estate was not worth the trouble. Samantha hoped not.

At any rate she intended to use some of her own fortune to pension off a few of the older servants, as it was doubtful that Phineas had taken their long years of service into consideration. Never a generous man when alive, it was unlikely that he remembered them properly in his will. Samantha even had hopes of weaning some of the more desperate tenants from their predilection for free trading. If only she could think of a way to provide gainful employment for them . . .

It was obvious when Samantha finally reached her bedchamber that Jenny and Robert were finding the extra company a burden, as the grate in her fireplace was still clogged with coals from the previous night. Dropping to her knees, she began to clean it out herself when Bunch discovered her.

"Miss Samantha, get up off that floor this instant. Tending the fire, indeed! If your mother, God rest her soul, could see you now, the dear lady would swoon!"

"I did not know she was one to faint so easily, Bunch. You always said she was so brave."

"And that she was, following your father to all sorts of heathen places. If she hadn't gone to Italy with him where the food is enough to poison a body, she'd be alive today."

"A carriage accident could happen anywhere." But the unconvinced woman sniffed eloquently, letting Samantha know just how much that bit of logic weighed with her. "You had better get out of that old dress before the new master sees you."

"He has already seen me and made his sentiments

clear. You should be quite pleased to know that he finds my workaday role just as unsuitable as you do."

"Sounds like a sensible man to me."

Samantha gave the affronted nurse a warm squeeze. "Be patient, Bunch. Soon we'll be out of here and I'll hire all the maids you like. Even one to help you light the fires."

"And I still say you're daft to spend your youth hidden away in a cottage with an old woman like me. You should marry the new master and stay here."

"He hasn't proposed yet," Samantha reminded her dryly.

"If only you'd take that silly cap off your head and get some decent dresses, the idea would come to him in no time."

"How uninspiring to have a gentleman fall in love with your wardrobe. Oh, don't look so fierce. I'm just going to finish this mending before I change. Is Mr. Ponsoby down yet?"

"He's closeted himself in the library this half hour past, but the others are still abed. Your Aunt Dakins don't get up before noon, you know." The nurse shook her head in disgust. "Come here and make you wait on them hand and foot when they weren't even invited. I'll wager the master didn't leave them a farthing."

Samantha perched herself in the window seat of her room with the pile of mending beside her. Bunch should only know how right her predictions were. Last night Mr. Ponsoby had requested that only the two beneficiaries be present for the reading of the will. That announcement sent Mrs. Dakins off on an orgy of recriminations. Why hadn't Phineas left even a token bequest for her children? It was the height of ingratitude, she declared vehemently. But the lawyer calmly reminded her that since she hadn't been contacted at the time of probate, she had no reason to think her family would be legatees.

Bunch was still mumbling to herself about certain people who butted in when they weren't wanted as she folded away Samantha's freshly laundered dainties, but all in all the old nurse was quite happy. For the first time Bunch was confident that with a little push here and there from wiser heads, Miss Sam was on the road to happiness. As for her mistress's plan to live in a cottage near Brighton, Bunch gave that scheme about two months.

Soon Miss Sam would be hobnobbing with the *ton*, and quick as Bob's your uncle, she'd be married. Bunch sighed with pleasure at the thought of getting back to her own proper work, loving and cosseting little ones. No doubt about it, that money was going to change things around for Miss Sam, at last. The girl might be convinced, thanks to her grandfather, that a plain, colorless spinster was doomed to life's leavings while prettier girls got their pick, but Bunch was determined that Miss Sam should have it all: high society, pretty clothes, and most important, a fine husband. The nurse already had her eye on a likely candidate. It would be perfect, she thought happily. And no one would have to bother to move.

CHAPTER 4

Mr. Ponsoby had elected to read the will in the gloomy chamber known as the library, although Phineas had never been a great reader, and the few shelves of books there had been ordered *en masse* from a bookseller in London thirty years before when the Pillars was first furnished. There was the distinct smell of mold and a hint of mouse in the dank air as the diminutive lawyer fixed a lusterless eye on the two heirs.

"This is a painful duty, Miss Crawford, Major. I have done my best over the years for this estate, but Phineas Crawford was a hard man, a man determined to go his own way." Mr. Ponsoby's face betrayed some emotion, at last, and a faint flush entered his sallow cheeks. "I warned him many times, but it was no use."

Major Crawford moved impatiently in his chair. "Mr. Ponsoby, I gather you have something unpleasant to impart. Would you please come to the point?"

"Never mind my sensibilities, sir. I beg of you, read the will and let us be done," Samantha said with spirit.

"The will was made some fifteen years ago and never altered. I'm afraid it is hardly to the point now. Simply put, it leaves to Miss Crawford the investments in Funds. Major Crawford inherits the farms, the land, and the house."

Samantha leaned back in her chair and smiled. "Well then, it is just as we supposed. Congratulations, Major."

"But that is not all you have to tell us, is it?" the Major asked sharply. "Well, spit it out, man."

"Miss Crawford, you must have noticed that there has been a certain lack of luxury these ten years or more."

"Yes," Samantha agreed, a chill creeping into her heart.

"Did you not wonder that your grandfather refused to take you to London for your come-out?"

The Major was irritated. "Be done, sir, with your maunderings. What is it?"

Mr. Ponsoby sighed and looked pityingly at Samantha, spreading his hands emptily before her. "The Crawford fortune is gone, all gone. The panic on 'Change in June during the battle of Waterloo took the last, the very last. Your grandfather died penniless. There is only the Pillars, and debts. Quite a few debts."

Samantha sat soundless in her chair. Poor grandfather! He had let them all think him a miser and misanthrope. If only he had told her! For a moment she feared she was going to weep. She stood up. She refused to cry in front of these strangers.

But the Major was barring her way. "Sit down,"

he commanded. "Bring her some brandy," he growled at Ponsoby.

Samantha wanted to protest, but it hardly seemed worth the effort. She sat down obediently, eyes bent to the carpet, and found a glass pressed into her hand.

"Drink it," he ordered and she sipped a little, wishing the Major's solicitude were a bit less overwhelming.

"That is sufficient," she choked. "I am quite all right."

"I hope so." The Major took the glass away and looked at her keenly. "I'm afraid this has been a terrible shock to you. You have borne up bravely under it."

"Bravely?" Samantha essayed a smile. "I have not taken it in, I think."

"Well, you needn't worry overmuch. You will make the Pillars your home, and I will sign over some income to you after I have examined the situation a little. It is only fair; the old man would have changed the will if he had not been struck down so quickly."

The Major's voice was matter-of-fact, but Samantha was shaking her head. "He didn't intend to," she said clearly. "He told me, at the end, that the land was for you to carry on the line."

Ponsoby was looking pleased. "The Major has just made as fine an offer as I've heard in forty years."

"I cannot accept, of course," Samantha replied.

Mr. Ponsoby was taking a ridiculously long time

44

to read a simple will, but the Dakinses waited patiently in the morning room. Exasperation finally sent Amelia off for a stroll around the garden, leaving Elizabeth to listen with but half an ear to her mother's lamentations at Phineas's summary disposal of such a large fortune. Most of Anne's performance was for her son's benefit, to remind him that he still hadn't secured Samantha's hand. Jasper was well aware of his mother's conviction that were her dear sister-in-law alive, the Dakins family would have received their rightful share of the wealth. But since Sophia Crawford had despised her brother's wife as much as Phineas did, that bit of wishful thinking was merely a favorite fantasy of Anne's, though she had spent half a lifetime working toward that end, plaguing her widowed brother-in-law with unwelcome visits.

Yet it was really Samantha who benefited from that. She truly enjoyed the company of her cousins. Though Amelia was never a favorite, Jasper had been her companion on many an adventure. And if Samantha had taken the blame for his misdeeds on more than one occasion, she hadn't minded. Those visits were the only cheerful break in the monotony of her days.

Mrs. Dakins was resentful at being left out of the will, but she had already begun to comfort herself with the thought that Jasper would soon convince Samantha to marry him. He was a handsome, charming boy, Anne told herself, forgetting momentarily that he was also irresponsible and selfish. The heiress had turned him down twice, but she would

45

succumb eventually. For what more could Samantha hope? A girl with her obvious limitations.

Satisfied that she was being more than fair, Anne now had a new scheme to occupy her, bringing the virtues of her eldest daughter to the attention of Major Crawford. A man of wealth and distinction, he would make an admirable son-in-law.

It was nearly one o'clock before the sound of the library door opening brought Mrs. Dakins into the hall. Samantha, looking remarkably unhappy, passed by without a word while the Major watched her disappearance up the stairs with a stern expression on his face. Sensing disaster, Anne clutched his coat sleeve before he too could disappear.

"Major, what is it? Samantha seemed so . . . so . . ."

Sighing resignedly, he explained the situation as briefly as possible before removing her fingers gently from his coat and stepping back into the library.

Anne stood staring at the closed door for a few mindless seconds before hurrying back to the morning room. It would never do. Jasper must be informed immediately.

"What is it, lovey?" Bunch asked in alarm, seeing Samantha's white face as she entered the bedroom.

"There's nothing, Bunch." In a colorless voice she went on to explain. "Grandfather was destitute. He sunk every penny he had on some wild speculations. The panic on the Exchange this June finished him. I suppose it was that news that brought on his stroke. The estate is heavily in debt."

46

"But—but—I don't understand." The old woman looked distraught. "What about your legacy?"

Samantha took a deep breath. "I have no legacy, dear. The Crawford fortune is gone. The only thing left is the Pillars, and Major Crawford must spend a small fortune himself to keep it together."

Samantha was still in a state of shock. Of all the explanations for her grandfather's parsimony, the most obvious had never occurred to her.

"There is nothing for you?" Bunch could not seem to get it through her head that all their dreams and plans were useless now. She blinked back tears of disappointment. If Miss Sam could be brave, then so could she.

The two women looked at each other in growing dismay. What would happen now? Where could they go, an old woman, crippled with rheumatics, and a young one with a very sketchy sort of education?

A knock at the door interrupted them, and Jenny peered in nervously. Already the word had spread that Miss Samantha was no better than a pauper, and the Major was left with the old man's debts.

"Mr. Ponsoby wishes to see you privately, miss."

Samantha gave a sigh of resignation and followed the maid back down the staircase. Mr. Ponsoby was still lodged behind the heavy oak desk in the library, his mass of papers ready to be restored to their proper place in the locked green boxes behind him.

Samantha sat with her hands folded in her lap. The worst had happened. There was nothing more he could say.

Ponsoby cleared his throat. "I have taken the lib-

47

erty of speaking to Major Crawford again, and he has been most generous in reiterating his offer to you of a permanent home at the Pillars. He feels as I do that a young lady should not be forced to leave the protection of her family. Your, ah . . . rash words should be reconsidered before you make any final decision."

"Tell the Major thank you, but no."

"Miss Crawford, how can you think of going out on your own when your home is open to you? The Major is well able to do his duty. Besides, your efforts these past years in running the house ought to make you realize how useful you can be. I'm sure your grandfather counted on the Major's sense of responsibility."

If anything were needed to stiffen her resolve, those fateful words would have sufficed. "My mind is made up, Mr. Ponsoby, and I am depending on you to help me in this matter. I could be a companion. I have experience, you might say, with old people. Or I could teach. I'm not very good at the pianoforte, but my French is passable. You must know some respectable family."

"Then you won't change your mind?"

Samantha rose to her feet and said with more firmness than she really felt, "Mr. Ponsoby, believe me, I am appreciative of the Major's kindness, but I cannot accept his charity."

"Charity! My dear girl," the lawyer was appalled, "it is not charity to carry out one's family duty."

"I don't wish to be the Major's duty, Mr. Ponsoby. He has too many others to fulfill. Putting the Pillars back on its feet will be no small undertaking."

Samantha hesitated a moment, then said with difficulty, "I had hoped to help out in some way myself. A few small loans . . ." She shook her head. "But now, that too is out of the question."

Samantha thought unhappily of the small cottage in Brighton to which she and Bunch had so looked forward . . . and the loan for Jasper's horse farm. As for the tenants . . . well, that was a problem she'd have no chance of solving.

"That's very generous of you, Miss Crawford," the lawyer said in some surprise. "Of course, you realize you are hardly in the position to maintain yourself, much less help anyone else. You would do well to accept the Major's offer."

But Samantha was adamant in her refusal, and Mr. Ponsoby left with the promise that he would look into some sort of employment for her.

Samantha would have been content to spend the rest of the day in her room to avoid the pitying gazes of the others, but Perkins made a special trip upstairs to coax her down for dinner. It wouldn't do any good to hide away like a criminal, Bunch admonished, and the family had to be faced sooner or later.

Samantha acknowledged the truth of that statement, but it didn't make it any easier. Donning her black silk once again and schooling her face to what she hoped was a calmly dignified expression, she presented herself in the dining room.

It was an awkward meal, and everyone was relieved when the last dish was removed. The Major appeared preoccupied and hardly listened to the desultory conversation around him. He had found himself in a coil and could see no way out. From his brief ride this morning, the appalling conditions of the estate were clearly visible. The woodland hadn't been cleared in twenty years, and many of the saplings were being slowly strangled by the decay. The few cottages he passed showed signs of neglect, and healthy fields lay fallow. Even the once lucrative Crawford stone quarry was worthless now.

According to Ponsoby, it would take a small fortune to put things right, and since Wyndham possessed only a moderate competence, he was finding it difficult to see how he could correct these ills. If he were to sink the capital needed into the Pillars, it would leave him practically without means.

Then, too, there was the matter of smuggling. Mr. Ponsoby advised him that many of his tenants were involved in the illicit practice of free trading. It seemed to be the only paying work a man could find. The Major had no trouble believing that after what he had seen of conditions on the estate. If he were to accept the burden of this legacy, that was just another of the problems he would have to remedy.

But none of them were any more troublesome than what to do about Miss Crawford. Today's revelations seemed to come as a complete surprise to her, though in retrospect one could say that she might have guessed that things were not as they should be at the Pillars. How still she had been when Ponsoby broke the news. No outcry at all, though Wyndham would not soon forget the stricken look in her eyes. Damn it all, the lawyer could have had the decency to warn her! Actually it was no one's fault. That miserable old man had allowed her to believe that she would be independently wealthy and treated her shabbily in the meantime.

The Major admired Samantha's courage, though he deplored her intention to seek employment. It was sheer bravado, no more. Once the shock of her changed circumstances wore off, and she realized the truth of her position, his offer of hospitality would, no doubt, be reconsidered. It was still too soon to expect her to think rationally, he supposed. Though if she persisted in her foolishness, something would have to be done to convince her of the impropriety of her plans.

Jasper also was wrestling with a problem. It was one thing to ask his cousin to marry him when he thought she was to inherit a sizable income, but things were rather different now. He told himself that she had turned him down quite definitely last night, yet he knew in his heart that if he cared a button for her, he would ask her again. Dash it, he was fond of her, but he wasn't so cursed anxious to saddle himself with a penniless wife, especially one for whom he could feel only a brotherly affection. Nevertheless he eyed her uneasily, half expecting her to tell him that she had changed her mind. If she did, he'd have to say that his offer was withdrawn, and that would be damned uncomfortable.

Amelia, quite aware of her brother's predicament, watched the byplay with interest. "Tell me, Major, how do you expect to repair the family fortune?"

"I'm afraid that will have to wait until I have a chance to study the situation."

"The Pillars turns out to be not quite a honey fall, eh?" Jasper commented meanly.

"Now, children," Mrs. Dakins scolded. "I'm sure the Major will put things right as soon as he is able. After all, it was not his fault that the market tumbled."

"*Crashed* is the word, I think," Jasper corrected with a quick look at the Major.

"Well, I think it's terrible that Samantha gets nothing," Elizabeth cried in real distress. "She's the one who had to live with that horrid old man."

"That's the gamble she took," Amelia taunted, watching the slow flush that rose on Samantha's cheeks. "It's a pity," she continued, "that Uncle Phineas didn't settle an income on her before he started speculating on the Funds. Of course, he could have been afraid that once she got her hands on a bit of money, Samantha might run off and leave him."

Elizabeth glared at her sister. "You know she wouldn't have left. Maybe you would have run off, but not Samantha."

"And look what she got for her trouble," Amelia retorted.

Their mother pushed her plate away petulantly. "I wish you two would stop bickering. Amelia, you sound positively unkind. What will the Major think of you? Poor Samantha is homeless now, and your attitude is not helpful."

"Miss Crawford is not exactly at the mercy of the cruel world," came the gruff voice from the head of the table. "I have offered her a home here."

"And I have refused that offer."

"You refused?" echoed Mrs. Dakins in disbelief. "But, my dear, it is quite a munificent invitation under the circumstances."

"Haven't you heard, Mama? Our Samantha is going to become a governess," Amelia announced in dulcet tones.

"Listening at doors again, sweet sister?" Yet Jasper couldn't help but feel relieved. That certainly let him off the hook. But a glance at Samantha's set face was an uncomfortable reminder that a scant twenty-four hours ago he had offered himself in the role of protector to her.

Mrs. Dakins was clearly distressed. "You can't become a governess, Samantha. What would the family think?"

"What family?" Jasper asked. "Ain't that us?"

"And your opinion is already quite apparent," the Major remarked dryly.

"Don't like the idea," Jasper flushed, "but what can she do?"

"Stop it!"

All eyes turned to Samantha at that outburst. Her cheeks held two attractive spots of color, and her blue eyes sparkled with annoyance. Calming herself with some effort, her angry gaze flew to Wyndham. "There is no need to discuss this any further. Mr. Ponsoby is making arrangements on my behalf, and I hope to begin looking after myself very shortly."

"But, Samantha," Elizabeth cried, "it's awful being a governess. You'd hate it. And what about poor Bunch? Weren't you going to set up house with her?"

53

"Don't concern yourself with Miss Bunch," the Major interrupted. "She has agreed to stay on at the Pillars."

Samantha felt betrayed. Bunch hadn't said a word to her about it. "Why are you doing this, Major?"

"Your grandfather was unable to provide for her, so it falls upon the estate to see to her needs."

"But the estate is you," she protested.

"And that leaves me free of its obligations? Come now, Miss Crawford, you can't think so ill of me as that."

Samantha wondered helplessly if Mr. Ponsoby had suggested this, but then decided it was merely the Major's rigid sense of duty that had prompted the offer. Only now Samantha felt adrift. Wherever she went, it would be alone, without even the comfort of her nurse's presence.

Reading her expression accurately, Wyndham suggested that they all adjourn to the blue salon. Miss Crawford's reaction to his announcement was not the one for which he had hoped. With nurse Bunch remaining, he expected her capitulation to follow. Was she hoping Jasper would rescue her? Surely she could see from his hangdog air that it was useless to expect anything from that quarter.

He stopped her at the doorway of the drawing room. "Miss Crawford, I suggest you reconsider. Give yourself time to think things over carefully. And don't look to young Dakins to save you."

"I don't expect anyone to save me, Major. Many women have been forced by circumstance to work. There are worse fates."

"You think so?" He rocked on the balls of his feet. "You are a proud woman, Miss Crawford, and a governess, even a companion, must forgo that luxury. I fear you will have a difficult time of it."

"Perhaps not so hard. And at any rate it is preferable to the role of dependent."

"Damn it," he barked, "you're an obstinate woman. You'd do better to heed me. Is my help so hard to accept?"

"Your charity, you mean, Major? Yes, it is."

He watched her walk away from him, an angry frown marking his brow. She was too cool, too controlled. Women are supposed to swoon in the face of adversity and be grateful for the generosity of a stalwart gentleman. Miss Crawford was in for a harsh awakening. Governesses are not allowed a prideful air. She'd be taken down a painful peg or two if she kept up this manner.

He followed Samantha into the room and found a seat near the window. Pouring tea as though she hadn't a care in the world, he thought grimly. Well, she'd learn.

No sooner was everyone settled with their hot drinks than Perkins was called to the front door by an insistent knocking. It was rather late for a visitor, and the entire company listened as an imperious voice was heard rapping out commands over the furious barking of what sounded like an entire pack of wild dogs.

The wide, gilded doors of the blue salon were thrown open with a flourish, and Perkins announced in stentorian tones, "Lady Hester Fitzcameron."

The bearer of this title swept regally into the room, followed by two black-haired, snarling Chows. A large purple turban clashed violently with her unlikely red hair, while her lined and withered face confronted the startled company in haughty grandeur.

Mrs. Dakins's face blanched noticeably when the crackling voice rapped out, "You here, Anne? Haven't worn out your welcome yet?"

"Hester!" she squeaked, reaching for her vinaigrette and waving it feebly about. "What are you doing here?"

"Swore I'd never set foot in this place, but now that Phinney's dead, I've decided to change my mind."

"Who is she?" whispered Elizabeth.

"This, my dear girl," smiled Major Crawford as he stood up to greet the visitor, "is 'the Family' to whom your mother referred. The dowager of the Crawfords, the matriarch." He bowed and raised her gnarled hand to his lips. "How d'you do, Lady Fitz. You're just in time to sort things out." He threw a speaking look to Samantha.

"Don't try to turn me up sweet, boy. It won't do you any good. Now which one of these namby-pamby misses is the granddaughter?"

CHAPTER 5

The incorrigible Lady Hester Fitzcameron breezed her way into the Pillars and within two days was not so much a guest as in command. It didn't take her long to measure up the situation and rearrange everything in a more proper fashion. She immediately instructed Wyndham to hire some additional help, then conspired very cleverly with nurse Bunch to set them about their duties with little help from Miss Crawford. Wyn, the dear boy, made no protest; but Samantha was, at first, rather stubborn about surrendering the domestic reins to more menial hands. Her resistance was eventually worn down, but it was no easy task to wrest away the habits of a lifetime. Samantha rather thought she could detect the heavy hand of Major Crawford in this new arrangement, though Phineas's sister needed little encouragement to take charge in any situation.

Samantha felt an instant liking for the old lady, despite her managing ways. That seemed to be another trait the Crawfords shared. But Samantha still stung from the Major's sharp rebuke the other night.

Since then he had maintained a scowling but voiceless disapproval which bothered her not in the least. The Major was inherently dictatorial and possessed a naturally contentious disposition, but years of experience had taught Samantha how to circumvent that kind of male tyranny. She had always appeared submissive to her grandfather's autocratic rule, while quietly going her own way. She behaved no differently now.

True, her domestic duties were lightened, and somewhat against her will, but Samantha did not relinquish her prerogative of visiting the tenants and doling out advice on farming methods and livestock maintenance. She blithely assured them of the Major's full cooperation, then went right to the bailiff with her requisitions. That put Mr. Doolittle in an awkward position, as he could make no final decision without the Major's approval. But he hesitated telling this to Samantha, for the girl was still too used to issuing orders herself to adjust to the new state of affairs. So he kept silent and passed on the requests to Major Crawford as his own suggestions.

Keeping busy on the estate was also an excuse for Samantha to stay out of the house. Not that Lady Fitz wasn't an enjoyable companion, but remaining indoors also meant bearing the Dakinses' company, and Samantha was quickly growing out of patience with them. In the evenings, when they all met for dinner, Samantha had no choice but to observe how incessantly Amelia flirted with the Major. What irritated her more, though, was that after a week, the

Major hadn't found it tiresome yet. Hester finally brought it to an end.

Indeed, her routing of the Dakinses had been a masterful stroke. Last night, after yet another account by Anne of Phineas's lack of foresight, Hester could hold her tongue no longer.

"Don't bray like more of an ass than you really are, Anne. Phinney wouldn't have allowed you to get your rapacious hands on one sovereign of his precious money. He knew you too well. Look to your children if what poor Edward left you isn't enough. The boy might be capable of an honest day's work, and your girls are certainly pretty enough to marry well. All you need is a set of wealthy in-laws who'll put up with you."

That uncalled-for remark sent Mrs. Dakins into an aggrieved silence, and shortly after she retired to her room.

Samantha smiled guiltily to herself, yet she couldn't honestly say she was sorry to see her cousins leave. Amelia had slapped Jenny for some minor fault, making the girl run weeping to her mistress. Samantha calmed the maid, but only after promising her that she needn't wait on Amelia for the rest of her stay, an awkwardness that the new servants did little to alleviate, for Samantha found herself pressed into service to run the Dakinses' errands and listen to their complaints.

That state of affairs was woefully clear to Lady Fitz and uppermost in her mind when she made her brutal assault on Anne. It was ridiculous that Samantha should be run ragged by these pretentious upstarts. The girl was still in the habit of obeying their every whim, and they didn't have the sense or the consideration to cease treating her like a servant. In fact, now that Samantha's circumstances had changed, the Dakinses showed less civility than ever.

Samantha was grateful that Hester had managed to dislodge the Dakinses, but it certainly showed the less amiable side of the old lady's character. That sharp tongue was surely the reason she and her brother had quarreled so bitterly. Two such determined personalities were bound to clash. Neither had any finesse or subtlety, only an unshakable conviction that they were never wrong, a fault the Major shared as well. But while Samantha was always a little terrified of her grandfather, and annoyed by Major Crawford's high-handed ways, she found her aunt endearing. Behind Lady Fitzcameron's gruff manner lay a sentimental heart, and this less obvious side of her nature became more apparent to Samantha as the days went on.

One afternoon as they were about to partake of tea, Hester's lively pair of Chows escaped Jenny's watchful eye and came charging into the drawing room. Yapping and snarling, they chased each other around the delicately fluted legs of the Hepplewhite table, coming within a hair's breadth of dumping the silver tea service on the priceless Aubusson carpet.

"Lin Chi! Lan Toy! Stop that, you bad dogs! Lord, give me strength. They'll be the death of me yet. Samantha, be a dear and get them away from me."

Samantha, after ringing energetically for Perkins,

tried unsuccessfully to capture one of the furry brutes as it careened by and tangled itself in her skirt.

Perkins took in the situation at a glance and held the doors of the drawing room wide. "Come, Lan Toy, Lin Chi. Shall we see what Cook has for you?" he inquired politely.

The dogs paused, ears aprick, then bolted through the open door and headed down the stairs, sounding amazingly like a dozen large elephants rather than two rather small Chows.

Puffing heavily, Lady Fitz sank gratefully onto the silk brocade daybed. "Dreadful beasts! I think I'll have them put away. Oh, fetch me my vinaigrette, Samantha, do."

Samantha chuckled and offered her great-aunt the comfort of her smelling salts and fan.

"And you needn't laugh, miss! If they had knocked over the tea table, it would not have been amusing."

"Why, Aunt, you seem out of patience with your darling doggies. And they are such dear little creatures," Samantha said demurely, a wicked twinkle in her eye.

"I hate 'em," Lady Fitzcameron admitted gloomily. "Nasty, dirty, little things. Sly too. Notice how they toad-eat Cook? That's because she feeds 'em chicken livers and who knows what other absurdities?"

"Well then, why do you keep them?" Samantha asked reasonably. "I'll admit they made a superb entrance with you when you first arrived, but since

61

then I've hardly seen them. I know you bribe Jenny to keep them away from you."

"My husband, John, gave them to me. They were my last gift-from him, and so sweet when they were puppies. Oh, don't ask me. One of these days I'll have them shot. But perhaps not today. Well? Are you going to sit there and smirk at me forever, or do I get some tea?"

In addition to rearranging Samantha's duties, Hester showed a sympathetic interest in everything that went on at the Pillars and, of course, found a willing ally in nurse Bunch. The two of them took great satisfaction in picking over Phineas's many faults.

Bunch had given Lady Fitzcameron a highly colored account of the latest events at the Pillars, complaining justly of the treatment accorded Samantha.

"He always was immensely selfish," Hester agreed with relish. "I begged him to send me the girl years ago, but the old monster insisted he needed her. How like him to make a mull of things. Lost all his money and, from what I hear, didn't even have a good time doing it!"

The Pillars was taking on a fresh vitality with the addition of Major Crawford and Lady Fitzcameron to the household. Their presence created a more lively and demanding regime for the servants. Perkins, who felt that the main rooms of the house were his territory, was soon forced to yield to pressure and begin training Robert to help serve in the small dining room that was reserved for intimate family meals.

It took fully a week before Perkins declared the young footman ready for his debut, and even then it was evident that the boy still needed a helping hand. While Perkins hovered in the background and filled the serving bowls, Robert offered the vegetable platters. His nerves were not what they might have been under less trying circumstances and in a moment of clumsiness he dropped the serving spoon. The distraction caught him off-balance for a moment, and forgetful of the proper procedure, he bent to pick it up. This, of course, upset the delicate equilibrium of the tureen of rhubarb in his hand, and the contents spilled over, narrowly missing the Major's fawn waistcoat.

It was then the Major earned the boy's undying devotion by apologizing for his carelessness in knocking Robert's arm, and without another word the mess was cleared away.

Despite that contretemps, the house was running quite smoothly. Surprisingly it was nanny Bunch who had stepped into the picture. With the encouragement of Lady Fitz, she took on the responsibility of supervising the raw young maids in their duties, creating yet another change not altogether relished by Samantha.

But Miss Crawford's biggest complaint was not being done out of further responsibility. Her frustration was at the Major's lack of good sense in not coming to her for advice. Why wasn't he taking advantage of her vast experience? The complex details of running an estate this size could not be mastered in a few short days. Was he so conceited that he thought himself capable of any undertaking, or was he just too proud to admit that he was at a loss?

Samantha neither knew nor cared, but her resentment increased as the days sped by, and the Major continued to ignore her, except for uttering a few civilities at the dinner table. His complacency was galling. But he would learn. Samantha only hoped that it would not be at the expense of the tenants.

Meanwhile Lady Fitzcameron was also displeased at the way things were going. She had not lightened Samantha's workload only to give the child a well-deserved rest. In fact, Hester was quite annoyed that Samantha was not taking better advantage of her free time. Deciding that a little push was needed to get things going, Lady Fitz summoned Samantha to her for a serious talk.

Holding court in the large drawing room, Hester prepared herself for this interview by donning a pink gown with bon bon sleeves and a narrow skirt set with rows of red ruffles. All of this clashed dreadfully with her hair, and although Samantha thought she had grown accustomed to her aunt's more bizarre impulses, the sight of a paper rose perched rakishly on top of the orange curls made her blink in astonishment.

After a few moments of one-sided conversation Hester led into her purpose with typical verve. "So, you still insist on the nonsensical scheme of finding employment."

"I should be hearing from Mr. Ponsoby quite soon."

"You must know I don't like the idea."

64

"I'm afraid there's no alternative."

"Fiddle! What do you know about being a governess?"

Samantha launched into an account of her abilities on the pianoforte and with watercolors, adding for good measure that she knew French conversation, a little Italian, and the rudiments of Greek and Latin.

"A blue stocking, eh? I always said your grandfather was a fool."

"You flatter me, Aunt. But I do know enough to teach young girls. However, Mr. Ponsoby is also looking out for a position as companion. I have plenty of experience for that," she said with asperity.

"You should stay here," Hester insisted.

"That is out of the question."

". . . and marry Wyndham. That is the only reasonable solution."

"Don't you think the estate has enough liabilities, Aunt, without the Major saddling himself with a portionless wife? I can well believe that it might not appeal to him. And what about me? Do my feelings count for nothing?"

"Romance is a luxury you can't afford, my girl. Besides, Wyn knows his duty."

"I am well aware of his feelings about duty, Aunt. But you certainly can't put marriage in that category."

"If it's that monkey, Jasper, you're after," Hester said suspiciously, "I wash my hands of you. Why turn up your nose at Wyndham Crawford? He's got a fine army record."

"If I were a general, that recommendation would

no doubt convince me," Samantha answered. "Isn't this a rather useless conversation, Aunt? The Major hasn't offered for me and isn't likely to."

Lady Fitzcameron wasn't about to accept that as defeat. "Then I shall speak to him about it."

"Don't you dare. Now behave yourself and inform Bunch the same applies to her. Obviously the two of you have gotten your heads together over this." Samantha ended the interview by saying she had promised to confer with Cook about tonight's dinner, and she left her aunt temporarily silenced.

It was difficult to be angry at Lady Fitz's sincere attempt to see her settled. The thought was touching, really. Except for Bunch, no one cared what became of her. Yet her aunt's suggestion was totally preposterous. The Major had not shown the slightest interest in her so far, except to insist she stay on as a sort of pensioner, and the idea of being the poor relation, dependent on this arrogant and short-tempered man, was totally abhorrent to Samantha. They didn't even like each other.

Wyndham had just returned from a meeting with the bailiff when Perkins informed him that he had a visitor. Stepping into the library, he was engulfed in a crushing bear hug.

"Stacey, old man! I thought you still in Belgium. What brings you here?"

The large bulk that comprised Captain Eustace Trumbull, in the dashing uniform of the Light Bobs, lowered itself into a massive leather armchair, an engaging grin splitting his large face in two. "I've sold out, Wyn. There's nothing left to do in Europe but kick one's heels around headquarters, so I've decided to become a civilian. It seems to suit you. A gentleman of property, no less."

"That remains to be seen. At least there's an adequate wine cellar." Wyndham poured two glasses of excellent French brandy to prove his claim. "Will you be going into the family business now? I hear industry is the one sure thing in our battered economy."

"No doubt about that," his friend said with feeling. "But to tell the truth, I haven't any plans at the moment . . . except to enjoy my freedom."

"An excellent idea," Wyndham laughed.

The two of them drank to the Captain's future and spent a pleasant hour recalling their more notable moments together. Stacey readily agreed to prolong his visit as he was keen to sample the delights of the countryside. His huge frame set a horse well, and he enjoyed some mild hunting if the distances weren't too far; his bulk tended to tire a steed quickly. Promising him a variety of pleasures, Wyndham went off to arrange a room for his guest.

That was the first Samantha heard of a visitor, but after some swift mental calculations, she had Cook add four partridges and a rack of lamb to the evening's fare, and when she saw Stacey, she was glad she hadn't stinted. A six-foot-four titan of a man, his overwhelming physique was softened by a pair of light brown eyes and an engaging disposition. A gentle giant, Samantha described him to nurse Bunch.

The Major made no mention of the changed

household arrangements to Samantha, and she refrained from telling him that it took the better part of an hour to prepare the green room for his guest. Unused since Mr. Ponsoby complained of its oversized bed, it was the only room in which Captain Trumbull could hope to rest comfortably. The furniture had been among the few pieces salvaged from the old manor house, and only then because Phineas declared that Queen Bess herself once passed a night in the great bed. The green velvet coverlet was threadbare and worn in spots, but a lace throw hid the worst from view.

In keeping with country hours they sat down to dinner at six, and in deference to the Major's guest, Perkins put them in the large dining room.

Captain Trumbull entertained his hosts throughout dinner with a lively account of his adventures in Spain, carefully edited in due respect to the ladies. Wyndham expanded under his friend's cheerful raillery, showing a fine sense of modesty as he disclaimed the more heroic deeds attributed to him.

If his friend could be believed, the Major was an extraordinary man: brave, intelligent, and responsible. Samantha hoped it was true, for those virtues would be needed by the master of the Pillars. It would take every ounce of strength he could summon up to put the place on its feet again. She had noted the grim set of his mouth every time he rode out to inspect the various parts of the estate and the forbidding look he had on returning. It was an overwhelming task. The bailiff told her that to clear the mortgages alone would take years . . . and luck.

Samantha would have liked to be a part of that effort, but she would never sink to the point of setting her cap for the Major. Such a distasteful notion was beneath her dignity. As for Hester's insistence that Major Crawford was duty bound to offer for her, Samantha dismissed that as the farradiddle it was. He would laugh himself silly at the notion.

Of course the thought of staying on at the Pillars was appealing; this was the only home Samantha could clearly remember. But leave she must . . . and soon. It was just a matter of time before her uneasy relationship with the Major blew up into an argument. And Samantha abhorred uncivilized conduct.

CHAPTER 6

The Major had left the house early this morning, and Samantha took advantage of his absence by ordering the two new gardeners to dig up the weeds on the south lawn and replace the herbaceous border that once grew there. She had already instructed Bess, the girl hired to clean the top floors, to air out the unused bedrooms and, with Robert's help, to wash the windows in the east wing. Now Samantha went to seek the bailiff and put a few more matters straight. He was in his office behind the stable, his bald head bent over a ledger.

"Good morning, Mr. Doolittle."

"Oh, Miss Sam. I didn't hear you come in." His moon face beamed with pleasure at the sight of the girl he had known since she was a babe.

"I see the Major has given you your fill of paper work."

"True enough, but he's gone over most of it himself. A very thorough man."

"I'm glad to hear that. But when I rode by the Huddle farm yesterday, it was deserted. He didn't evict them for nonpayment, did he?"

"Never, Miss Sam. But you know how bad the roof is there. The Major moved them to the empty Baker place."

"He did? How enterprising. It saves him the cost of a new roof."

"Now, Miss Sam, don't you go thinking that. The Huddles like it where they are. The Baker place is bigger, too."

Not wanting to, but feeling he must, Doolittle told her also just how pleased Alf Huddle was to be away from his ramshackle place—what with the smugglers using his barn at odd hours, and not leaving more than a penny's worth of tea behind. Thomas Doolittle had little sympathy for smuggling, but he couldn't deny the hold it had on the locals. He even wondered if Alf was one of them.

"Then I suppose it's for the best," she sighed. Bringing herself back to the business at hand, she reached into her skirt pocket. "I have two pounds I can easily spare, and I want you to give it to Ben Gates. His oldest, Harry, starts work at the tailor's shop soon, and the boy hasn't a decent shirt to his name."

"Now, Miss Sam . . ."

She did not give him a chance to argue. "And do not tell anyone that I had a hand in it. It's best if they think it came from the Major."

"I couldn't do that," the bailiff protested. "Major Crawford would be most displeased if he knew."

"Well then, don't tell him. It will be our secret." Samantha put the small stack of coins on his desk and fixed him with a pleading eye. "You and I know it's little enough. What we really need is something that will give employment to everyone in the neighborhood."

"That's not your responsibility, miss, but it's like your kind heart to care." Doolittle sighed and proceeded to pocket the money. The habit of obeying his erstwhile mistress was still strong, though his expression showed plainly what he thought of her action.

Thomas Doolittle would have been doubly dismayed if he had known just how short of cash that meager gift left Samantha. But she comforted herself with the knowledge that she would soon be employed and in the position to do more. Fortunately neither governesses nor companions were expected to dress in the height of fashion, so her rather shabby wardrobe would do well enough for another year.

Walking back to the house, Samantha thought of the fruitless letters she had written while her grandfather was still alive. He never knew she had applied to a textile mill in the Midlands about using the woodland for furnace fuel, but since coal was the cheaper source, they had turned her down. She'd even petitioned the navy about buying the wood for shipbuilding. Now that the war was over, there was little likelihood of that either. The farmland could reap an income, but improvements had to be made first, and even then it would take years to show a profit.

Thinking wistfully of the days when the quarry guaranteed everyone a comfortable living, and no one had to resort to smuggling, Samantha entered the house in search of her nurse.

It was smuggling, oddly enough, that provided the topic of conversation after dinner that evening. Lady Fitzcameron had chosen to shock her audience by repeating some of the more scandalous stories about the earlier Crawfords, who demonstrated a marked penchant for bending the law to suit their pocketbook. The original Crawford fortune owed its origins to privateering, she announced. Penn Crawford sailed with Drake against the Spanish armada and caught the attention of the royal household, receiving a large grant of land as his reward. His pretensions to respectability were soon tarnished by his rakehell son, William, who seduced a lady-in-waiting and fell out of royal favor in consequence. One of his sons, in turn, was rumored to be the infamous highwayman, Black Jack, but no one was ever able to prove that claim since the rascal was hanged before he could be identified. Families were larger in those days, and a missing son went more or less unnoticed. One Crawford built a tunnel from the manor house to the cove and conducted a highly lucrative smuggling ring until he was forcibly put out of business. In fact, Hester claimed with pride, it wasn't until the quarry was opened that the family made the least attempt at a respectable enterprise.

"A foolhardy venture," the Major said facetiously. "But this is the first I've heard of a tunnel. Is it still in use?"

"Do you mean for smuggling, Major? I don't think anyone has stepped foot in the place since Jasper and I played there as children," Samantha told him. "Are you thinking of reopening it?" she asked lightly.

"Smuggling is not such a farfetched idea," Hester mused. "You must admit, no Crawford was ever intimidated by the rules of convention."

The Major held up a protesting hand. "Smuggling's been illegal these two hundred years, and I don't condone it for the sake of a little untaxed wine."

"Pooh, everyone turns a blind eye to it in these parts," Lady Fitz scoffed. "Why, I well remember when I was a girl how welcome was the occasional keg of French brandy left on the doorstep. My father appreciated a gift from the 'gentlemen.' "

"I don't think we get any such gifts these days, Aunt. Smuggling must not be so prevalent as it used to be. Does that set your mind at rest, Major?"

"I'm not so sure, Miss Crawford. It is rumored that the practice flourishes hereabouts."

"I've heard those rumors, too, but should you heed them, sir?" she asked earnestly, the note of lightness quite gone from her voice.

"If you're not careful, Wyn," his friend broke in, "you'll have the ladies thinking you some kind of laggard."

"Never that," he smiled.

"I'll have you know," Stacey went on, "that Major Wyndham Crawford stood up with the great Jackson himself. He could have made a fortune in the ring if he weren't a gentleman."

"You mean fisticuffs?" Samantha asked in surprise.

"That shocks you, Miss Crawford?"

"Not really. The Major has the look of a man who

74

can take care of himself. Only I doubt that it will help him to repair the family fortune . . . unless he decides to set up in competition to Mr. Jackson."

Her last words held a glimpse of humor that the Major found very engaging. Miss Crawford was adept at turning a quick phrase when she wasn't remembering to be so prim and proper. He immediately responded. "I fear the bloodthirsty tastes of our forebears have found a kindred spirit in you, Cousin."

"Not at all," Samantha informed him in mock gravity. "But I do claim a touch of admiration for their sense of business."

"What a splendid combination," Lady Fitzcameron applauded. "Samantha's astute practicality, and Wyndham's sense of adventure."

"I daresay they'd make a great team," Stacey agreed. "But couldn't they channel their efforts into something less strenuous? Not fisticuffs or smuggling. Why not reopen the quarry?"

"I'm afraid not, dear boy. That market was exhausted long ago," Hester sighed.

"There must be something left," he insisted.

"The builders use brick these days. Our limestone is worthless," Samantha told him.

"Not all of it is worthless, Miss Crawford. If it's limestone, there's a great market for it." He turned to Wyndham. "I told you about my brother's venture in Kent. He uses limestone in making his Roman cement."

"You mean that imitation stone?" Hester scoffed. "I saw some in London, and it cracks as soon as the

75

weather changes. Lady Devon had quite a time with it when she decided to redo her terrace garden. Not dependable at all," she stated autocratically. "No, I fear the quarry is useless to these children."

"The quarry has nothing to do with me, Aunt," Samantha reminded her.

"Only if it could restore your inheritance, my child, and I fear nothing can do that now."

Samantha could not but agree with her aunt's prophecy.

Early the next day Samantha received a note from the Major desiring her presence in the estate office "at her earliest convenience." Samantha read the curt missive and looked up at Robert in surprise. "He wants to see me now?"

"At your earliest convenience, ma'am," Robert repeated woodenly.

"Perhaps there is some difficulty with the tenants and he needs my advice finally. Well, I am more than willing to come." Samantha put away her embroidery and headed for Doolittle's office with a glad heart. She had been longing to talk to the Major about the problems of the estate, and he had evidently realized at long last that his experience as a soldier had not equipped him for the onerous task of land management.

Even as she crossed the cobbled yard, the Major, dressed in riding breeches and a leather waistcoat, swung open the door to the office. "Come in, Miss Crawford. Sit down. I have something to say to you. Something you are not going to enjoy hearing."

Samantha looked a question, but contented herself with sitting in the proffered chair. The man was clearly angry, but Samantha was getting used to his uneven temper. Silence was the best defense, she decided as she awaited the explosion.

"Your interference in the estate management has come to light, Miss Crawford. And while I believe that you have nothing but the best of intentions, it must cease—immediately."

"Interference? What can you mean?"

"Oh, let us not play games, madam," he replied with heavy irony. "I've been receiving reports for days now, and this morning, when I went by the south lawn to check on the gardeners' progress, they told me you had instructed them to discontinue reseeding and begin planting an herbaceous border. That is contrary to my wishes. A flower garden would only attract the birds, and I want to protect the saplings in the adjoining wood from them." He leaned over the desk and glowered at her. "Then Doolittle confessed."

Samantha looked at the bailiff, standing red-faced and sweaty by the window. "Under threat of torture, I'm sure. But what harm have I done? I apologize about the gardeners, but surely a little charity here and there is within my province."

"Nothing is within your province, Miss Crawford. Let us understand that now. You should have seen fit to come to me first."

"This is not a battlefield, Major, nor are we your soldiers. I do not recognize your right to order me about." Samantha was angry but her voice was cool and composed. "You would do better to accept my help. I have lived here nearly all my life, and I know what is best for the Pillars. But because I am a woman, you have ignored me."

The Major smiled grimly. "You made it clear from the first day that you resented my presence. I am not one to beg help where it is not offered."

Samantha's lips opened in surprise. He thought that? Because she had refused to ride out with him that first morning? Because she refused his charity? "I do not resent you," she denied in the face of his open skepticism. "How can you think it?"

"Because it is true," he said succinctly, folding his arms across his chest and looking steadily at her. He fully expected her to begin raging at him, but to his deepest annoyance she only appeared even more in control.

"I know you are the heir, Major, but I am still a Crawford."

"Then why, when I offered you an income from the estate, did you refuse it?" he snapped irritably.

Samantha raised calm eyes to his stormy gray ones. "You will need every penny from the land to put it to rights again. And I am capable of supporting myself."

"What you mean is that you will take nothing from me. Not even what is yours by right—a home here." The Major spoke harshly, incensed by her calm negation of his criticisms.

Samantha was on her feet. She would not stay to bandy words with this impossible man. "I will be gone soon, sir. Until then, I will endeavor to remember that the Pillars is yours and yours alone."

The Major saw nothing but a cold, proud woman in front of him, but Samantha was almost overcome with rage. Resent him? How could she help it? He was so arrogant, so sure of himself. A typical army man, all ramrod back and barking voice. As for his offer of a home at the Pillars, she'd rather starve first.

It took an hour of strenuous walking over the hills to the sea before she could calm herself. When she returned to her room, it was with a renewed determination to leave the Pillars. A letter to Ponsoby was posted that afternoon. In it Samantha demanded that he help her find employment. Now!

She made no secret of her actions and stood fast even against Hester's dictum that she recant her foolish decision. That forced Lady Fitz to put her plan into effect sooner than she anticipated.

A few days later the Major was sitting at his desk in the somber library, his eyes reluctantly drawn to Samantha's graceful figure as she worked in the rose garden. The sun shone on her fair hair and kissed a hint of color into her pale cheeks. He was lost in his own thoughts until a sharp rap on the hand brought him back to the present.

"A pretty picture, eh?"

Hester was dressed a little less elaborately this morning, allowing country custom to dictate a severe black lace gown with white ruching along the high collar. It might have been more in keeping with a morning call in the city, but she felt its severe lines were concession enough to local tastes.

"Good morning, Lady Fitz. Yes, it is a very pretty picture, but I'm not in a mood to appreciate it."

Seating herself in the plain wood chair across from the desk, she started in at once. "I have just concluded a highly unsatisfactory discussion with Samantha, and how she can grub about in the dirt as if she hadn't a care in the world is beyond my comprehension."

"What did she say to put your back up?"

"She insists on going through with her notion to find employment."

Wyndham matched the old lady's fierce expression. "Did you really expect her to change her mind? I would have thought you knew the girl well enough by now."

"I have used every argument I can think of, but she is stubborn to the point of idiocy."

Wyndham smiled mirthlessly. "No more so than you, dear lady. I remember how you took my side when I wanted to buy a commission in the army. My mother was set against it, and you convinced her otherwise."

"That was common sense, my boy. It was obvious that you were cut from the same cloth as your father, and a braver man I never knew. If you had stayed in, you would have made general. Even your mother, were she still alive, could have no objection to that. But you are a landowner now."

"You mean this cursed inheritance."

Reminded of her reason for being here, Hester became plaintive again. "Cursed is right. Samantha is beyond me. I can only think of one solution to her problem, and that is for you to marry her."

"Ha!" he laughed grimly. "She can't bear to be in the same room with me."

"Nonsense." Hester was outraged. "She likes you well enough. You're both Crawfords, that's all. A little temper on both sides can be the spice of life."

"I have the distinct impression that Miss Crawford would prefer anything to a life with me. She says she wants her independence. So let her have it," he said sourly. "Much good may it do her."

"Independence?" Lady Fitz snorted. "She won't have much of that as some horrid child's governess. Slavery is more like it."

"I remind you that she has an alternative. I have offered her a home at the Pillars, and she doesn't have to marry me to get it. But she's made up her mind that it is charity. And she says she won't take orders from me, either."

"Of course not. No woman likes to be told what to do. But if you'd make a bit of a push to woo her, she could be brought to her senses. The girl's not a fool, Wyn, even if she acts it. She knows which side her bread's buttered."

"What! Buy myself a wife? I am not so desperate. I may be a scarred old soldier with no soft words to please the ladies. Still, I have my pride."

"A commodity the Crawfords never seem to lack," Lady Fitz exclaimed in exasperation.

"You forget, Miss Crawford has her eyes on another gentleman," the Major pointed out.

"If you are referring to that jackanapes, Jasper,

then disabuse yourself of the notion. Samantha has no interest in him."

"That isn't my impression. On the contrary, her interest seems quite marked."

"That is immaterial. He'll never marry her, for all her foolish notions."

"I hope for her sake that you are correct. Nevertheless she isn't a child, and whatever her decision, she's quite capable of carrying it out."

"I don't question her capabilities, only her sense. Is she to slave away her youth as some cranky old woman's companion?"

"No doubt the stubborn chit will do as she thinks best. There's no point in our worrying about it."

But while the Major was able to fob off Lady Fitz with those nebulous words, he was not above doing a little worrying on his own. Samantha Crawford was undoubtedly the most stubborn woman in all creation: irritating, proud, interfering, and provokingly independent as well. What would happen to her when she got out into the wide and indifferent world was anyone's guess. Nothing very pleasant, the Major was sure. His eyes searched the garden for the slim figure in gray, but no one was there.

CHAPTER 7

A cold wind tore around the protecting ridge that fronted the shore, and whipped across the flat promontory of land where the old house stood, its back to the sea. A solitary horseman galloped at breakneck speed toward the house, only to turn at the last moment and disappear quickly over the brow of the ridge. Damp hoofprints in the long grass remained as evidence of his passing, but the wind and the screaming gulls were once again the sole occupants of the deserted landscape.

Not long after, a second rider came trotting up the same overgrown path but reined in his mount as he reached the edge of the spinny. It was his first unbroken view of the old manor. Quieting his nervous beast with a gentle hand, he studied the abandoned house with interest.

Sturdily built, the manor nevertheless showed the effects of forty years neglect. There was a brooding melancholy in its shuttered windows and a sense of desertion in the litter of roof tiles that had blown to the ground. Untended yews flanked the windward side of the house, and the walled garden, once sweet with kitchen herbs and roses, had become a rank and jungly growth of bindweed and brambles.

Touching the mare's tender side with a spurred heel, Major Crawford urged his unwilling steed toward the front entrance, but Lady rolled her eyes and danced uneasily as if the old manor held some spectral presence visible only to her equine eye. The massive oak door that had weathered two hundred years of wind and rain and sea-born gales looked ready to withstand as many more. No easy entrance here for the casual passerby, Wyndham thought, reluctantly giving up his half-formed plan to explore the house's interior. That would have to wait for another day.

Instead he studied with interest the stone walls of the house that were built from the same rock found in the long-abandoned Crawford quarry. Once a profitable venture, according to Ponsoby, and a source of income for owner and laborer alike, the quarry was closed when the market for stone dwindled as bricks became easier and cheaper to use in the building trade. By then the Crawford fortune was no longer rooted in local industry, but spread out in far-flung investments in many other countries.

Yet it was the quarry that brought Wyndham riding out today. His curiosity was aroused by the conversation with Stacey, and he wanted to see for himself in what condition it was. Perhaps his friend would understand better, but it looked to Major Crawford as if it were beyond reclamation. The sides were overgrown with weeds and fern, and the bottom seemed to be a jumbled mess of rubbish. Ponsoby was probably right that there was nothing to salvage there. Phineas wouldn't have overlooked the slightest thing. He as well as the locals could have used its benefits in recent years, for when the quarry closed, everyone had to look elsewhere for a living. It was understandable why free trading held such an attraction for the men.

Smuggling had always been a part of life along the coast of England, but with the embargo on French goods forcing up the price, and the gentry's taste for French brandy as insatiable as ever, it became ever more richly rewarded. Even respectable householders closed their ears to the sound of a laden wagon rumbling by at midnight and received a coveted length of lace or a chest of tea for their silence.

More recently the fear of French invasion and efforts to control the flow of treasonous information had resulted in a severe enforcement of the regulations and the stepping up of patrols along the shore. The excisemen may have turned a blind eye to much in the past, but no longer. Too many French spies had wangled their way across the Channel, and the King had ordered the watch increased. Even now, with Boney vanquished once again, the patrols continued, and the tariffs were as high as ever. Smuggling was a high-risk business conducted by desperate men, and there was no shortage of such in the country these days. Soldiers, home at last, were finding honest work hard to come by. Worse, the new Corn Laws, designed to protect England's wheat farmers, had driven the price of bread to ruinous heights. There were riots in the Midlands and hordes of hungry, ill-fed folk in every parish.

How could one man hope to correct things when he hadn't the faintest notion of how to begin? That thought bedeviled the Major as he circled toward the back of the manor house to the spur of land that jutted out over the sea. He stared into the waves that leaped and frothed against the white chalk cliffs as though he would find some answer there.

Curious, he dismounted and walked to the land's rim. What kind of smugglers could have used this treacherous place? A crazy Crawford to be sure. But when he looked down again, he noticed that the curve of the beach here was really a cove. The infamous tunnel must lead to it, he thought. It was truly a perfect spot for an unauthorized landing. That ancient Crawford should be congratulated for seeing the possibilities that nature planted on his own doorstep.

Splattering raindrops brought his musings to an end, and the new heir to the Crawford estate turned wearily to his patient mount.

"Well, Lady," he said, patting her glossy neck, "let's go home."

The lane he had chosen meandered in slow loops across the hills, while the gentle rain turned the dust to mud that balled on the mare's hooves. Wyndham glimpsed the Pillars once in the distance, but for the last ten minutes the twelve-foot-high hedges on either side of the rutted country road effectively blocked his view. Standing in his stirrups, he searched vainly for a familiar landmark, but the lonely road lay too deep in shadows for him to know if it led in the right direction or not.

Rain was dripping uncomfortably down his neck when he sighted a farm wagon turning the bend toward him. "Hello there. Can you tell me if I'm on the road to the Pillars?"

A man bundled in a patched greatcoat, his stringy hair flattened by the rain, drew the wagon to a halt and stared up at the Major. "Lost, are ye?"

"I'm new to these parts and haven't my bearings as yet. Is this the right road?"

"Yes, it am, Squire," he grinned knowingly, showing a line of yellowed teeth.

"Are you one of my tenants?" Wyndham asked, certain he hadn't seen him around here before.

"Nay, gov'ner. Just passin' through, though I'd deem it an honor to work for ye."

Not liking the man's insolent grin, Wyndham thanked him shortly and started off down the lane again, but as the wagon lumbered past and out of sight, the Major paused to look back. There was something oddly familiar about the man, though for the life of him Wyndham couldn't imagine where he had seen that unpleasant face before. Shaking off the nagging feeling that the man somehow knew him, he urged Lady to a canter and soon passed through the tunnellike lane into the open expanse of parkland.

The rain had eased slightly by the time the laden farm wagon reached the manor house, and the burly man in the patched coat took his time to scan the area for prying eyes before emitting a low whistle.

The side door opened, and a petulant voice called

out. "What took you so long, Pargins? I've been waiting over an hour."

"Did the new Squire see ye? I jist passed him on the road."

"I came in by way of the tunnel. He didn't see anything."

"Good for you. 'Cause if he did spot ye, the deal's off."

"You can't back out now. Besides, I'm the only one who knows about the tunnel."

"So ye do. Now lead me to it."

"Just a minute. How do I know you won't back down after you've got what you want?"

"I want a safe place to work from, and ye want to become a free trader. That's fair enough. There ain't no contracts in this business, Mr. Dakins. Take it or leave it."

"What about Huddle?"

"What about 'im?" His new place is too out of the way to be any use, but he's still one of us."

"All right," Jasper conceded. "Follow me."

CHAPTER 8

Jasper turned up at the Pillars on the following Tuesday late in the afternoon and found Samantha in the rose garden. The cutting shears were in her hands, and the last of the year's blossoms made a colorful show against the gray muslin of her dress. Jasper was quick to flatter.

"A rose among the roses—sweet Coz!"

Samantha brushed a fallen curl from her forehead and gathered together the last of the cuttings. "Very pretty, Jasper, but I'm covered with thorns. Be careful." Grasping his outstretched hand, she pulled herself up, scattering rose petals at her feet. "These sunny days are a nice reprieve before the cold rains of autumn are upon us. What brings you here, Jasper? Certainly not a discussion of the weather."

"Exactly that, Sammie love. One last fling while the sun is shining. A picnic, no less. Amelia wants an uninterrupted day with the new heir, and how better to impress him with her charms than against the background of falling leaves and prickly nettles?"

"Do I detect a certain cynicism in your attitude?"

Samantha queried as she peeled off her gardening gloves.

"I feel a certain sympathy for any poor blighter Amelia snares. She'll lead him around by the nose, no doubt. But I am entirely in favor of this project. Tomorrow, while Amelia dazzles the gallant Major, I'll be free to roam the dells with you."

"To what purpose, Jasper? I warn you, if it's another loan you're after, I'm down to my last farthing."

"How mean of you to suspect my motives. Believe me, my heart is pure . . . or reasonably so. Let's be children for a day. I'll wager I can still climb a tree faster than you. What say you? Tomorrow? Please? Amelia won't forgive me if I fail her."

It sounded to Samantha as if Amelia were pursuing the Major in earnest. While the prospect of being witness to her stratagems was not especially pleasing, the idea of a picnic did seem inviting.

"Famous," Jasper smiled at her assent to the scheme. "Your guest, Captain Trumbull, can entertain Elizabeth." With that offhand sorting of partners, Jasper followed her into the house and lost no time in presenting the outing to the Major as a *fait accompli.*

Lady Fitzcameron thought the idea of a picnic silly on a crisp October day, but nevertheless lent her energies to insuring its success. Taking the menu out of Samantha's capable hands, she decreed that nothing less than an epicurean feast would do. And if Samantha was awed at the choice of delicacies, Cook was aghast. In addition to stuffed partridge and rolled filets of beef, there would be tiny ham balls, seed cakes, a lobster salad, sliced peaches, and four bottles of legally stamped French wine. In her only concession to practicality, Lady Fitzcameron allowed a flagon of lemonade to be added. The preparations thus completed, the weary lady took to her bedchamber for a well-deserved rest, saying enigmatically that since it was a family outing, Wyndham and Samantha required no chaperon.

The picnic was to be at the Folly, a covered arbor that had been erected for use as a summer house. The latticework was broken, but the roof would still keep off the rain, and the floor was strong enough to hold their small party.

Robert was sent over early to sweep and refurbish it as best he could, and shortly after twelve o'clock the baskets of food were loaded into the back of the open carriage, while the three passengers squeezed themselves into the front.

The sun was shining as they started off, an auspicious sign that the afternoon was theirs to enjoy. For Samantha this outing was especially sweet. She was well aware that this might be the last of such carefree days for her, and she was determined to enjoy every minute. The necessity of earning a living would soon curtail such excursions.

The carriage passed beyond the manor, sitting in splendid decay at the crest of the hill, and turned into the narrow lane that led to the Folly. Some long-forgotten Crawford had erected this frivolous bit of architecture to duplicate a Grecian temple. As children Samantha and Jasper had played by its fountain and water nymphs, delighting in the slide down one particular marble arm. The statues were almost completely covered in green moss now, their flowing robes eroded by time and nature, but the magic of the Folly still remained. Protected from the harsh winds that tore over the cliffs, it nestled in its green haven of overhanging oaks and willows that managed to retain their foliage long after the rest of the valley was strewn with leaves.

The other guests hadn't arrived as yet, but Robert was there to greet them and unload the heavy food hampers. A table was spread with a snowy cloth, and bright cushions brought from the Pillars added to the cheerful comfort of the rustic setting.

Wyndham looked around with interest. "This is a charming summer house. It needs a bit of work put into it, of course."

He then turned an agreeable smile of approval on Samantha, causing her an unaccountable flutter of pleasure, which she determinedly ignored. She had not dressed for the Major's sake in any case, but she was aware of the vast improvement in her looks today. Taking Hester's advice, she had abandoned the grays and lilacs of mourning and chosen to wear a primrose muslin that accented her fair hair and showed off her graceful figure. The dress was not new, but Samantha had embroidered rosebuds on the hem and sewn fresh lace around the collar. Her color was high under the Major's speculative gaze as she showed Captain Trumbull the special beauties of the secluded dell and talked of the childish romps in which she had indulged.

At the sound of carriage wheels they turned to see a black landolet drawing up at the summer house. A vision in cherry red emerged, flashing a dazzling smile.

"Why, Cousin Wyndham. How are you?"

Amelia's annexing the Major as a relative drew an expression of annoyance from Samantha that no one noticed in the flurry of removing the two girls from the carriage. But Wyndham's greeting was warm, despite the unwarranted familiarity.

"My dear Miss Dakins, delighted as always to see you."

He took the fluttering little hand that hovered so uncertainly above the wrought-iron rail and escorted her up the two narrow steps to the summer house, as though it would have been impossible for such a slight creature to manage them on her own.

Amelia gave him the full advantage of her limpid green eyes. "Thank you," she murmured softly before lifting her hand from the strong arm supporting her. "Oh, my. The Folly is in shocking repair but wonderfully quaint, don't you agree?"

"I'll agree that your brother's idea to picnic here was inspired," he replied nicely. "But let me make you known to a dear friend of mine."

Stacey made a leg and Amelia dimpled charmingly at him, but it was Elizabeth, following on Jasper's arm, who held his gaze. Captain Trumbull stared wordlessly at this picture of perfection in pale blue dimity whose chestnut ringlets curled enchantingly under the brim of her chip straw hat. Elizabeth blushed furiously and cast her wide brown eyes down at this open admiration, then turned away in confusion as Stacey attempted to take her hand and stutter something resembling a conventional greeting.

Wyndham watched his friend's smitten gaze with amusement. Never a ladies' man, Stacey was finding it difficult to utter even the most common civilities to this shy, young creature who looked ready to bolt at the first provocation. It was Samantha who finally eased matters by asking Elizabeth to sit beside her.

Amelia, far from shy, clung to Wyndham like a limpet, taking great care not to leave his side even as they sat on the rug to eat. She praised the meal excessively upon discovering that it was Lady Fitzcameron who had arranged it, hinting that her cousin was far too nipcheese in her ideas to produce anything in such style.

Wyndham listened to Amelia's chatter with every evidence of absorption, but he couldn't help noticing just how outrageously Jasper was flirting with Samantha. And she appeared to be taking great pleasure from it.

Yet that was not quite so. Samantha's attention was not completely focused on the charming young man next to her. She too was distracted from her conversation, and the Major would have been most surprised to know that the cause of her unsettling sweep of anger was the way Amelia was playing the coquette. Samantha could have cheerfully slapped her when she "accidentally" brushed the Major's knee with her hand. The girl was displaying a shocking want of conduct. But the Major . . . he was positively relishing Amelia's improper behavior.

Samantha's temper was greatly improved when the exotic meal was consumed and Major Crawford left Amelia's side to join his friend Captain Trumbull. Her good will did not last overlong, as the Major soon began pinching another thorn in her tender side.

"Lady Fitz tells me that the old manor house was once a smuggler's haunt," he commented. "I did give the place a brief inspection, but it is in such deplorable condition, I wager our local lawbreakers have found greener pastures by now."

"Are there smugglers around here?" Elizabeth asked in distress.

"That's just talk, Lizzie," Jasper assured her. "Pay no mind to it."

"Then you are unaware that free trading is still a lucrative practice?" the Major asked. "Doolittle tells me it is a considerable business in these parts."

"Possibly," Jasper laughed. "But certainly not at the manor house. Have no fear, Major, no one in their right mind would take a chance on using that old barn of a place. There isn't a floorboard safe to walk on anymore," he scoffed.

"You seem to take free trading rather lightly, Mr. Dakins," Stacey said with a frown.

"I can't get excited over a few kegs of brandy coming in duty free. And those who enjoy the benefits don't strenuously object either. As for the blighters who risk their necks to satisfy the whims of the rich, what else can they do when Parliament all but takes the bread from their mouths?"

"These Corn Laws won't last," Samantha said

with feeling. "They can't, not when people are starving."

"I've heard there's rioting in the north," the Captain warned. "Let's hope it doesn't spread. You'd better watch out, Wyn. Hungry men can be dangerous."

"Surely not," Samantha exclaimed. "Our people are sensible and level-headed. They'd never turn on a Crawford. If only we could help them in some way . . ." Unconsciously her pleading eyes sought the Major's. Perhaps he would decide to sell the Pillars after all, she thought. Certainly no one would blame him if he did; it was a liability that could spell ruin. Yet somehow Samantha knew there was no possibility of the Major's discarding his inheritance. He was a man of honor, and he took his duties seriously, as she knew very well. Once he accepted an obligation, he would do his best to fulfill it.

As if he could read her thoughts, Wyndham answered, "I'm sure I'll think of something."

Bored with the conversation, Amelia suggested a stroll through the spinney. It was really only a small area, but the trees were thick enough to escape from the others for a short while. Soon everyone was up, agreeing that a walk would be pleasant.

Elizabeth shyly accepted Stacey's arm, the top of her head barely reaching his broad shoulder, while Jasper swung Samantha to her feet, and with a reckless laugh vaulted her over the short railing to the ground. She gave a breathless exclamation and brushed away a curl that had come unpinned. The two cousins wandered down a leaf-strewn path and

96

were soon out of sight of the others, but Jasper's mood gradually darkened. Sitting dejectedly on a fallen log, he began to prod the ground mercilessly with his stick. "Damn it all."

"What is it, Jasper? What's wrong?"

"Everything," he growled. "Oh, what's the use. You can't help; Mother can't help." And he pursed his mouth like an aggrieved little boy denied a treat.

"So it's money again." Samantha's voice held a note of exasperation. According to Perkins, Jasper had been frequenting a gambling hell in Brighton. He must have gotten in over his head.

"Of course it's money," he grumbled. "I tell you, Sammie, without some capital, I'm at a stand. That stud farm, I must have it. O'Toole says he can't wait any longer."

"I thought you'd given up that idea."

"I might as well for all the help I need. Damn it, I can't spend the rest of my life in this hole."

For once Samantha had to agree with him. Bored and aimless, Jasper would end up owing his life to the duns if he didn't do something rash instead. The horse farm was exactly what he needed, but it seemed an impossibility.

"I could go to Crawford for a loan," he mused darkly. "After all, he might end up my brother-in-law."

Horrified, Samantha protested. "Don't be a fool, Jasper. Have you no pride? He won't loan you money on the vague possibility of his marrying Amelia. Besides, he needs all he has to restore the Pillars."

"The hell with the Pillars! What's it to you if the whole place falls down? Don't you care about me?"

Shaken at the intensity of his feelings, Samantha said quietly, "Of course. It is none of my business, after all. You must do as you think best."

Jasper was a picture of despair as he rose and stood over Samantha with one raven lock of hair falling picturesquely over his frowning brow. "I have no choice. It's either Crawford or I turn to smuggling." As he posed, he watched for her reaction to his wild statement, but Samantha's sympathy was worn out by now. She knew him in his fits of melancholy and had no patience with them.

"Smuggling, indeed! It looks like rain, Jasper. Let's go back."

Sullenly he offered his arm, no more the lighthearted playmate with whom she had started this idyll.

The darkening sky brought everyone back to the shelter of the Folly, but as the rain held off, they lingered, chatting over the last of the wine.

Refusing an additional glass, the Major walked a short distance away from the group to indulge in one of his infrequent cheroots. When Jasper turned up at his elbow, he was struck by the young man's apparent nervousness and gave him a more friendly smile than usual.

Taking heart from it, Jasper launched into his request without delay. "Major, I've decided to buy a horse farm."

"Congratulations."

Missing the irony in Crawford's voice, Jasper went

on to describe the land in Ireland, the fine Arab stock he intended to buy, and how such an investment would surely pay off in vast dividends.

"You are experienced in these matters?" the Major asked curiously, wondering how a penchant for betting on horses made Jasper an authority on breeding them.

"Well, not exactly . . . but my friend is, and in no time he'll teach me all I need to know."

"I wish you the heartiest success."

Jasper flushed slightly but held his ground. "That's the problem. I promised O'Toole five thousand pounds to buy in. At the time I thought there wouldn't be any problem about the money, but since then the situation has changed."

Wyndham flicked an ash on the ground and waited. He had been expecting something like this. Since Samantha was no longer in a position to help her cousin, the boy was bound to turn to him sooner or later.

Jasper knew what the Major must be thinking, but there was no time to worry about pride now. Things were closing in on him. He had received word last night that a French trawler was due next week, and suddenly his deal with Pargins didn't seem so attractive. Smuggling was dangerous business, and the thought of it was beginning to frighten him. The Major was his only other hope.

"I thought since you're head of the family," he stammered, "I mean, Samantha's family, you wouldn't mind loaning me the money."

"No more than Miss Crawford would have minded, you mean?" the Major asked.

Jasper held back a sharp retort, knowing that a show of hostility would scotch his chances for good, but he longed to smack that supercilious smirk off the Major's face. "If I had any other recourse, I wouldn't come to you," he said stiffly.

For the first time Crawford had to grant the boy a grudging respect. Jasper was sincere and obviously at his last prayers to come to him, but inexperienced enthusiasm was almost a guarantee of loss in any business venture.

"Had you thought of working for a few years to gain some firsthand knowledge before launching out on your own?" This was said with utmost good will, but Jasper understood it as a refusal.

"You're a real Crawford, all right," he said bitterly. "I'm sorry to have bothered you." And with that he stalked back to the chattering group in the summer house.

Wyndham almost called him back, but Samantha had already noted the strained look on her cousin's face and was offering him a glass of wine. She truly cares for him, the Major thought as he tossed away his half-smoked cheroot with a bit more force than necessary.

Slipping away from the others, Amelia quietly appeared beside him under the partially concealing willow. "I hope you aren't angry with Jasper," she pleaded prettily.

"What makes you think that, Miss Dakins?"

"Well, I couldn't hear you, but my brother looks

100

none too cheerful just now." Her eyes followed the Major's glance to the couple now chatting amiably in the summer house. "Perhaps you were giving him good advice. He hates that. But never fear, Sammie will have him out of the sullens in no time." A quick look at the austere expression on the Major's face, and she continued her far from artless prattle.

"I suppose you can tell that she and Jasper like each other very well, but both of them are much too poor to marry. I feel quite sorry for them," she sighed sympathetically. "It's all her grandfather's fault, of course."

The note of condescension in Amelia's speech grated sharply, yet what she said was only what he thought himself. "Shall we join the others?" he offered politely.

Samantha consoled her cousin as best she could, yet it was painful to her too that he had humiliated himself for nothing. She knew Jasper was grasping at straws, for the Major would never consider such a proposal. But she did him less credit than he deserved in this instance. Major Crawford had by no means made up his mind about Jasper's request. On the contrary, he intended to find out more about the boy's rumored diversions in Brighton. Possibly Perkins could shed some light on the situation. He seemed to know everything that went on in the family.

CHAPTER 9

A week later the long-expected letter from the lawyer arrived. It was brought to Samantha in the morning room where she opened it under the interested gaze of Lady Fitzcameron.

"Well, what does he say?" The old lady tapped her fan impatiently as the silence in the room lengthened. "Couldn't find you a post, eh?" she crowed, noting the grave expression on the girl's face.

Quietly Samantha handed over the letter. "On the contrary, Aunt. Mr. Ponsoby has found an ideal position for me. I shall see London at last."

The clawlike hand in its black mitten took the paper eagerly. Peering longsightedly through her lorgnette, she read the missive, then snorted in disgust. "And who is this Mrs. Featherston-Hornby of Bentley Place? Some cit with more money than manners, I vow. I warned you how it would be. Write Ponsoby at once and decline."

"No. I'm sorry, Aunt, but I must accept this post. It seems eminently suitable in every way. Mr. Ponsoby writes that she is both respectable and pleasant. It seems foolish to expect more."

"It will not do, Samantha. Give up this mad scheme, I tell you. It reflects on the family if you go to a stranger to earn your bread. If you are so determined to be a companion, be mine. Crotchety and difficult I may be, but I have your interests at heart. I am lonely, and you would be a great comfort to me."

Samantha gazed in surprise at the shriveled but erect figure of her great-aunt. Somehow, despite her age, Lady Fitzcameron seemed neither lonely nor pathetic. Was her self-sufficiency a facade, then? Susceptible as always to the call of duty, Samantha asked, "You need me?"

"Not as much as you need me, girl. We'll get you some decent clothes, give you the London Season you should have had years ago, and I promise you a husband by next spring. How's that?"

"Why bother to ask me?" Samantha said. "It appears that you have it all worked out."

"Well, and what if I have?" the sharp voice demanded. "You're in no position to cavil, young lady."

Samantha, ready to yield at the thought of being both kind and useful, was firm against the imputation that she had no choice in the matter. "You would barter me off like some unwanted cabbage at the market."

Lady Fitz's mouth fell open like a startled rabbit's. "If I thought you meant that, I'd box your ears. You are a Crawford, remember. But perhaps that's the trouble; Phineas endowed you with his own colossal stubbornness."

Samantha refrained from answering because it was no more than the truth. Yet now faced with the results of her own brave words, she was beginning to realize the consequences of her decision.

Mrs. Featherston-Hornby might be only the first in a long series of invalidish old ladies, and a lifetime of fetching and carrying for strangers was hardly inviting. Nevertheless, Lady Fitzcameron's offer was equally distasteful. Samantha could imagine the embarrassment of being shoved into the Marriage Mart, as some wit had dubbed the London Season, where she would spend her time smiling at fatuous old men and lecherous young ones, sitting in corners at parties and waiting for the time to pass while younger and prettier girls whirled gaily by.

Of course, Lady Fitz would bully some poor dolt into offering marriage, a widower with a dozen unpleasant brats, or perhaps an elderly *roué*. Samantha couldn't fool herself into imagining that without a respectable dowry she would attract anyone really eligible. But marriage was never her aim anyway. She had looked forward to being independent. Now even that was denied her.

Perhaps Lady Fitzcameron guessed at the cheerless thoughts that bedeviled Samantha, for the fierce old eyes relented. "Well, if you won't let me do my best for you, I suppose you may still stay here. Wyndham would be happy for you to remain. And if you feel the necessity of earning your keep, there is certainly plenty for you to do. Wyn would be the first to admit that running the house is beyond him."

"You forget that Bunch has taken over. Besides,

I simply refuse to batten on the Major's hospitality any longer than necessary."

"You could make that hospitality turn into something more, if you chose."

"Not again, Aunt! Won't you forget that nonsense?"

"I never give up on a good idea, and no matter how you protest, marrying Wyndham's still the most sensible thing you can do."

"May I remind you that the Major has never shown any interest in me? Besides, I have a position now. I don't need his charity."

"How you harp on the Major's charity, Samantha. It's becoming a bore. Marriage is not charity."

"Really? Then why would he want to tie himself to a penniless spinster? It would be cheaper and far more sensible to hire a real housekeeper."

Offended, the old lady raised her lorgnette and eyed her great-niece frostily. "Cheaper, indeed! I am shocked at such a vulgar remark from you, Samantha. Believe me, Wyndham Crawford is no shopkeeper, and money is not the only consideration. You would make him a very excellent wife. You are, after all, a Crawford. And you are healthy, intelligent, and prettily behaved. Furthermore you would breed well, or I miss my guess. No, the heir to the Pillars could fare farther and do worse than you, my child. And it's time he set up his nursery. He is no youngster, as you well know."

Samantha had to laugh at that. "Healthy, am I? And would breed well? Now who is being vulgar?

Even the Major would find cause to blush at that testimonial, if he were capable of such sensitivity."

"You think so, eh? If you will allow yourself to be guided by me, it will all fall into place quite naturally. Wyndham would be justly flattered to be the object of your attentions."

"Surprised is more like it. Please, Aunt, forget about this matchmaking. The Major is not interested in me, nor I in him."

Hoping to pierce this smoke screen with infinite subtlety, Lady Fitzcameron covered a ladylike yawn. "Don't you like him? Even a little?"

"I think he is a very commendable soldier. After all, he was on Wellington's staff."

"Oh, you . . . begone. I've had enough of your fooling. If you refuse to be practical, then I wash my hands of you."

"Dear Aunt, I do appreciate your kind intentions, but you must let me live my own life." Samantha gave Hester a rueful smile. "That is the most practical thing of all."

Captain Stacey Trumbull had departed for Kent soon after the picnic to see his brother and settle a few family affairs. But within a week, lured by the memory of chestnut curls and shy brown eyes, he was back at the Pillars. Wyndham was delighted, of course, and if he had a shrewd idea that it wasn't the pheasant shoot that brought the Captain back, the master of the Pillars was too kind to tease his guest by alluding to the gentle giant's lovelorn condition.

Stacey was still in his room unpacking when the

sounds of approaching horsemen brought him to the window. Below him, under the jutting portico, the riding officer of the preventives dismounted and climbed the steps. Stacey heard the peal of the bell as the remaining troopers led their horses around to the back. Only mildly curious, he returned to his unpacking, and it was almost an hour later that he glanced out again to see the line of blue uniforms making their way down the front drive.

The Captain hadn't long to wait for an explanation, for at dinner that evening Wyndham announced that he had agreed to help His Majesty's excisemen in their efforts to clamp down on smuggling in the area.

Nodding his approval, Stacey saw Samantha grimace in distaste. "You don't like the idea, Miss Crawford?" he asked in surprise.

"I don't know. It seems rather heartless to help those old men in Whitehall when it is their fault that things are at such a sorry pass."

Halted in the act of slicing a large roast beef, the Major glanced over at her. "I know you can't approve of breaking the law, no matter how unfair certain government policies seem to be. What happens to the families of these men when they are caught and either hanged or transported?"

"Yes, that's just what's so unfair. But at least when they smuggle, they have food on the table."

"There are alternatives to a life of crime, Miss Crawford."

"Starving. It's not very appealing to most men."

"Surely you exaggerate. I realize that conditions

are hard these days, but before you accuse me of being a callous landowner, let me assure you that I'm aware of the difficulties."

"Are you, Major?" Samantha asked pointedly, her tone indicating otherwise.

"I think I'm tolerably well informed, Miss Crawford. And I seriously doubt that this neighborhood is very different from others. Unfortunately the entire country is in the throes of an economic depression. Still I say, smuggling is not the answer. That is why the King has so many preventive officers in his employ."

"Do you have an answer?"

"I hope to in good time," he replied soberly.

But Samantha was not appeased. Though the Major might have good intentions, his stern principles precluded accepting any excuse for unlawfulness, no matter how extenuating the circumstances. He had no sentimental attachment to these people nor any sense of duty toward them. That meant that Huddle, Mopes, and who knew how many others, were in great danger of being caught and exposed. With a hardened soldier like the Major actively working against them, they didn't stand a chance, Samantha feared.

Despite her native optimism, Lady Fitzcameron was very nearly discouraged. Her attempts to seduce Samantha from her path of self-sacrifice were unavailing. Wyn, too, remained irritatingly oblivious to all her machinations. But the old lady was not one to sit idly by and let a good plan fail. What these two children needed was a change of scene so they could come to appreciate each other. With the Prince Regent in Brighton, that pleasant resort might be just the place. The cause of romance would never be furthered amidst all this wrangling about smugglers and Wyn's sudden infatuation with his pestiferous quarry. Why, the two children scarcely saw each other. It was no wonder they refused to fall in love. And in spite of their immense good sense, neither Samantha nor Wyndham would budge one inch without some encouragement.

By now, too, Lady Fitz knew enough about Samantha to appreciate that the girl never refused a request for help. So using all the devious ploys at her disposal, Hester set out to smooth the path of true love.

It was in the morning room a few days later that she set her trap. After scanning a rather boring epistle from her cousin Araminta who lived in the outer reaches of Oxford with an equally boring spinster friend, Hester crumpled the letter into a ball and reached for her vinaigrette with an anguished moan.

"I can't believe it. No, no. It's too impossible." She sniffed the evil-smelling brew with unflinching self-sacrifice, making a convincing show of distress, and Samantha was instantly at her side.

"What is it, Aunt? What's happened? Did you receive bad news?"

"This missive," Hester faltered. "It's from my man of business. Oh, I can't believe it." Then rallying herself, she took Samantha's hand and said bravely, "I know I'm a foolish old woman, but such dire news

. . ." She broke off to let one pathetic tear work its way down her cheek.

"Please, Aunt, tell me," Samantha implored, kneeling in front of the distraught lady. "It must be terrible. I've never seen you like this."

Without a pang of remorse Hester wiped away the fortuitous tear, marveling at her own capacity for deception. She even managed a tremulous smile. "I'm sorry, my child. I've distressed you unduly. It's nothing," she assured Samantha with an unconvincing show of bravery. "Truly." But her trembling fingers groped for the vinaigrette bottle again.

Fortunately Samantha didn't notice that the cap had been adroitly replaced, or that Hester sniffed with real pleasure this time.

"I ought to have Perkins send for your maid. If you won't tell me what's disturbing you, perhaps a quiet nap will soothe your nerves."

"*No!* I mean, no, dear child. That's completely unnecessary. A little wine, perhaps."

Samantha filled a goblet to brimming with the restorative, which her aunt imbibed with every evidence of enjoyment. It was almost as if she were making a toast, and Samantha was filled with admiration for Hester's indomitable spirit.

Setting the empty goblet aside, Lady Fitzcameron patted the cushion next to her and bade Samantha to sit. "There. Now I feel more like myself. How silly to fly into the boughs over a bit of nonsense. Maddens always was a ninnyhammer about money, but then, I suppose that's what a man of business should worry about. It saves me the bother."

"Even so, Mr. Maddens would not subject you to such distress without reason. You haven't lost . . . everything?" Samantha asked with embarrassment at broaching such a delicate subject.

"You silly child. Only your grandfather could be such a gudgeon." Sensing Samantha's withdrawal, Hester once more took on the cloak of martyr. "No," she sighed, "the damage is not irrevocable, but it does mean I shall have to speak to Maddens personally."

"Then it's simple," Samantha replied with irritating logic. "Just have him come here."

"Ah, yes . . . but no. He can't come here. He's an invalid."

"Then how does he conduct your business?"

"From his bed."

Even Samantha couldn't be that gullible, and hastily Hester went on to explain that he only took to his bed on especially bad days. Most of the time he held regular hours, but because of the precarious state of his health, a long trip was out of the question.

"No, I must go to him," Hester sighed. "Although I fear the journey to Brighton might be too wearing on my nerves just now. The shock, you understand."

"Of course," Samantha soothed. "Can't it wait until you're feeling more the thing?"

"I'm afraid not. Business before pleasure, you know. That is if I can afford any more pleasure once the East India Company fails."

"The East India Company? Oh, Aunt, half the country will sink if that goes."

"I know, my dear, but we must be brave. I still have my jewelry, after all."

Horrified that Lady Fitzcameron might be put into the position of selling off her lovely pieces, each with its special sentimental significance, Samantha felt like crying herself. It was so unfair. "Is there anything I can do to help?" she asked with prompt predictability.

"The support of loved ones is always comforting in trying times," Hester declared mournfully. "But I couldn't ask you to accompany me. That would be too much."

"Ask me anything, dear Aunt. I can't bear to see you so unhappy." Samantha's heart was truly wrung by Hester's plight. She understood only too well how frightening was the lack of financial security. But if it could all be put to rights by a trip to Brighton, why such anxiety? It wasn't like Aunt Hester to fall apart so easily.

Then Samantha realized what her aunt's forceful personality made her overlook. Despite her dyed hair and brash ways, Lady Fitzcameron was an old woman. And like all elderly people, she feared being left alone and financially dependent upon the kind mercy of her remaining family. The Major was the only one capable of supporting her, and Samantha understood just how demoralizing that position could be. It wasn't the trip to Brighton that held any qualms for Hester, it was what might be disclosed once she arrived there. Painfully familiar with the anguish of such a revelation, Samantha was determined not to

112

let her aunt face the worst alone. And the post in London did not begin until next month in any case.

"I refuse to hear any objections," Samantha informed her aunt. "I am going to Brighton with you."

"Oh, my dear girl, such a noble sacrifice."

Hester threw her arms around Samantha in an unprecedented show of affection while Samantha patted her shaking shoulders consolingly and coaxed her to wipe her streaming eyes to partake of another fortifying glass of wine.

"It will be all right, dear Aunt. I feel sure."

"As long as you are with me, Samantha dear," Hester gurgled through the muffling folds of her lace handkerchief, "I know everything will turn out exactly as I wish."

CHAPTER 10

Brighton, growing in the sunshine of the Prince Regent's patronage, was in its glorious heyday in 1815. The simple fishing village of Brighthelmstone had been overlaid by sprouting rows of handsome town houses and fashionable shops. Only a few narrow and picturesque streets lined by ancient cottages recalled its past.

The wonder, some said shame, of this lively seaside resort was Prinney's fantastic pleasure palace. In the process of being redecorated by Nash to resemble some Indian moghul's residence, the Royal Pavilion burst upon the public with breathtaking exuberance. The new design was still far from complete, but the clear glass dome of the stables echoed the profusion of onion-shaped bulbs that topped the Pavilion itself. Lushly decorated and packed with treasures from the Far East, it was deplored by many as vulgar and showy, the perfect reflection of the Prince Regent's extravagant taste. Certainly the Pavilion was shocking to sensibilities trained to expect classical proportions and restrained elegance, but still there was both magnificence and a romantic willfulness in Nash's design that could not be denied.

Wyndham Crawford rode into Brighton at the close of a blustery October afternoon. The town was beginning to thin of company, and many of the houses were closed and shuttered. Prinny and his set were leaving for a shoot in Northumberland soon, and indeed most of the *ton* who were not foregathered in London for the Little Season were quickly scattering to their country estates.

Driving his curricle into the cobblestone yard of a small but spruce hostelry called the Red Lion, Crawford waited for Jem to jump down from his perch before releasing the reins to an anxiously waiting ostler. Almost instantly he was greeted by the host, a tall, red-faced man in a bottle-green coat with a soldierly set to his shoulders.

"Major! We're honored. Mistress Jellison has been in a fidget all day at the notion she was to meet you at last."

"How are you, Sergeant? But no need to ask. I see you are fit and well!"

The two men gripped hands as they grinned delightedly while Mistress Jellison stood in the background, smiling.

"Major, may I present my wife? She's that pleased to meet you, sir. Why, with the stories I've told her of the old days, she reckons she knows you as well as I do."

Mrs. Jellison, as rosy and rotund as her husband was lean, bobbed a curtsy. "Honored, I'm sure, sir," she murmured and ushered Wyn into a comfortable seat by the fire.

"Rum punch, Mistress Jelli," her husband ordered, and she bustled off, the picture of hospitality.

Wyndham stood warming his chilled back at the hearth and eyed the cheerful room. "You've found a snug retirement, Sergeant, no doubt of that. And your wife's clearly better than you deserve. I wish you happy."

Sergeant Jellison looked pardonably proud. "I've nothing to complain of, and that's a fact. How many an old soldier finds such a bolt-hole when there's snow on the roof and the wars are over?" And he pointed meaningfully to the grizzled thatch that framed his face. "Aye," he sighed. "I'm a lucky man."

Mrs. Jellison reappeared with a laden tray and put it down before the men. "Mr. Jellison, you do the honors," she said, beaming.

The Sergeant pulled a poker from the red-hot coals in the fire, blew off the ash, and plunged it into the punch bowl. Steam billowed as the scent of rum and spices filled the room. "It seems to me," he said with a mighty wink, "that a toast wouldn't come amiss just now. So if I could be so bold, let's drink to old comrades and old days, for they won't be soon forgot."

The Jellisons, though elderly, were mere newlyweds and clearly doted on each other. She'd been a lonely widow, saddled with an inn that was too much for her to handle. He'd been a thirty-year army man, newly retired with a bit put by for his old age. They'd met, discovered they hailed from the same West Sussex village, and wed as soon as the banns could be posted.

The Sergeant wrote the happy news to his commanding officer and learned on his side that the Major had sold out after inheriting an estate in the neighborhood. There was a good deal of respect and affection between the two men despite the difference in age and rank.

Years ago the Sergeant, a seasoned veteran, had saved a raw lieutenant named Crawford from making a mull of his first command. Later, as Crawford made his way, he kept the aging Sergeant near him.

Now, as the two reminisced, Wyndham was aware of a certain change in the relationship. As the host of a prosperous inn in Brighton, Jellison had taken a step up in the world. They were no longer Major and Sergeant, but two men with the memory of dangers shared, hardships endured together.

"Those were wild days, sir. I mind the time after Salamanca when the men went crazy with the glory of it. They were looting and drinking up that red wine like it was good ale, and we had to beat them into formation with our rifle butts, wondering all the time if they wouldn't turn on us like the wolves they'd become."

"I remember," Wyndham said, fingering his scar. "Wasn't that the time we broke a master sergeant for looting? He'd made a veritable business of fencing commissary supplies, too. What was his name . . . Jedidiah something or other . . . Parr, I think."

"Aye, and a black-souled scoundrel if there ever was one."

"Speaking of scoundrels, Jelli, perhaps you know a young friend of mine, Jasper Dakins. The rumor has it that he's been playing faro—and playing deep. Thought I might look him up."

"You won't have to look far," the Sergeant chuckled. "Happen he's staying here at the Red Lion. But I wouldn't have called him a scoundrel. Young and hotheaded, even silly, but not a bad'un, or I miss my guess. As to gambling, all the young bucks do it to their ruination. How can you stop 'em?"

"You can't. Still, his mother wants me to drop a word of caution in his ear. What sort of company is he keeping these days?"

"Well, I don't exactly keep track of all my guests, you might say. But I do mind that one time I saw him in my taproom with someone that surprised me a little."

"In what way?"

"The fellow was not a horse dealer. I can spot a tout a mile off, and your Mr. Dakins knows a few of those. Fond of the race track, he is."

"So what sort of man was he?"

"Sorry, sir," he said and shook his head regretfully. "I don't remember much except they had their heads together in the corner for over an hour, and I wondered, idlelike, what sort of business they could have together, a young gentleman and a shabby, middle-aged sailor."

"Hm, I see. At least there's no evidence of his being taken by a Captain Sharp." No need to tell

Jellison where his suspicions lay. "And where does Dakins play?"

"It would be Mrs. Lark's place. A house by the lanes in the old part of town. Quite a few of the young bucks go there regular. Not the most genteel establishment, but it ain't a hell neither."

The men enjoyed a pleasant hour together before Wyndham took his leave. Promising Jellison that he'd return soon, the Major proceeded to the house on Marine Parade that Hester had let for two weeks along with a retinue of servants. Only Jenny accompanied them from the Pillars, along with Hester's personal maid.

A very proper butler took the Major's top coat as he entered and informed him that Lady Fitzcameron and Miss Crawford had already left for a musical evening at the Draytons' house. "Lady Fitzcameron would be pleased if you would join them, sir. She told me that you were due to arrive at any time."

"Did she now? How optimistic of her."

"I beg your pardon, sir?"

"I take it a room is ready for me, then."

"It has been prepared for several days," Burns informed him with great dignity.

Wyndham followed him up the stairs and was ushered into a small but neat room that overlooked the street below. He bathed and changed out of his travel clothes into appropriate formal wear, although the Major's plans for the remainder of the evening had little to do with joining the gathering at the Draytons'.

Wyndham had responded to his aunt's compelling

missives, three, no less, to get himself to Brighton without further delay, assuming that she required his assistance on the highly secretive financial transaction that had sent her scurrying off almost a week ago. Leaving Stacey to continue his courting of the younger Miss Dakins, the Major set off, but halfway to Brighton he began to suspect that Hester's imperious summons had more to do with Miss Crawford than business. Her man of affairs was situated in London, if Wyndham remembered correctly. Perhaps Miss Crawford was balking at Hester's attempt to launch her into society, and that was exactly what Lady Fitz must be doing, he smiled to himself. Why else would she have cajoled the girl into accompanying her? Poor Samantha. She probably had no idea that her aunt could be so devious. Nevertheless the situation was ideal for the Major's purpose: an opportunity to find out just what young Dakins did with his time in Brighton. Perkins had started him on this train of thought, and the Major's suspicions were doubly reinforced by his talk with Jellison. That a boy of Jasper's limited resources could afford to be such a persistent gambler was remarkable, too remarkable not to look into.

That was the Major's intention when he presented himself at the door of number nine Grantham Street a short while later. Two smoky flambeaux illuminated the entry, and the front door was opened by an enormous blackamoor in scarlet livery. Flashing a mouthful of white teeth, the doorman ushered him into a large room filled with a noisy crowd of gentlemen in evening dress.

The high ceilings were luxuriously appointed with crystal chandeliers, while whist and faro tables were grouped underneath. Though there was no obvious drunkenness, a table of convivial youngsters laughed loudly over tankards of ale as serving men in livery circulated with trays of drinks.

Before the Major could do more than glance about, a woman in yellow silk rustled up to him, her daring décolletage as inviting as her provocative smile.

"Welcome, sir. I'm Mrs. Lark. Is your pleasure faro tonight, basset . . . or something . . . else?"

There was no mistaking the invitation in her blue eyes, and although past her first youth and well into her second, Mrs. Lark was an attractive picture. She had a partiality for military men, and the Major was a particularly fine specimen.

He took her proferred hand and smiled wickedly. "If my time were my own, madame, these walls would see little of you this evening, but I fear business must come before a very definite pleasure."

"What a shame, Major. I confess I've been longing for my bed these many hours, as the day has tired me excessively." She gave a delicate yawn to substantiate her claim, while the sparkle in her eye belied it quite expressively.

Crawford had decided that a *tête-à-tête* with Mrs. Lark ought to prove most enlightening, when his attention was caught by a group sitting at a faro table in the corner. Seven or eight men, their backs to him, were intent on the cards as the dealer, a pale, impassive individual, turned them over.

"Seven wins, gentlemen," he announced in a bored voice, while a groan of protest mounted, and a pile of chips moved inexorably across the green baize cloth.

"Damn, you have the devil's own luck tonight, Jas!" a young voice proclaimed enthusiastically.

Wyndham turned to Mrs. Lark with an apologetic smile. "If you will excuse me, I think I am in the mood for faro tonight, madame. I see an acquaintance at that table."

"Of course. And good luck." The hostess moved gracefully away. As long as a gentleman played and paid, she had no complaint, but she did give one regretful look over her shoulder.

Hands clasped behind him, Crawford took a position where he could watch the conclusion of the game. There were but three cards left unturned in the box, and bets were being laid on the order in which they would appear. Young Dakins had apportioned out his chips on the face cards painted on the cloth and waited the outcome with a brave show of nonchalance, though a pulse beat erratically in his neck, and the hand that fingered his loosened cravat shook slightly. There was a great deal of money on the table, and if the fates were kind, he would come away with a small fortune.

"Queen loses," droned the dealer. The rake came out and swept a monstrous stack of chips from the painted smirk on the Queen of spades. Moments later Jasper turned away from the table, forcing a choked laugh through pale lips.

"That cleans me out, Whistler. Come on, let's

drink to Lady Luck, though she is a jade. By God, I'm going to get drunk tonight!"

"Planning on drowning your sorrow, Dakins?" the Major asked, in his eyes both scorn and pity.

"Crawford! What are you doing here?" He looked with irritation at the immaculately clothed Major.

"Looking for you. Come, your plans sound . . . delightful. I'll join you." Wyndham smiled a touch sardonically, the white line of his scar twisting across his brow.

"The hell you say. And if I don't want your company?" Jasper's words were loud enough to cause a few heads to turn in their direction, and he lowered his voice. "What are you doing here? Spying on me?"

"Not precisely," Crawford answered evenly. "I was seeking company as I'm on my own tonight."

"Introduce me, Jas. Your manners are out," Jasper's companion spoke up.

Dakins glared suspiciously at the Major but muttered an ungracious introduction, and the two men bowed ceremoniously to each other. Wilfred Whistler, a fair, rather stout young man in a startling pink and puce striped waistcoat, suggested that they adjourn to the Spotted Dog, a tavern near the waterfront and only a short walk away.

"Excellent idea. An appropriate place to pursue the evening's program," Major Crawford remarked blandly.

In the process of shrugging on his overcoat, Dakins whispered fiercely to his friend that he was damned if he knew why he had to be saddled with

Crawford, a stiff-rumped, nipcheese fellow he abominated.

"Now, Jas, shut it up. It ain't like you to be so rag-mannered. What's the harm, I'd like to know?" his friend whispered back while the Major tried to pretend he hadn't heard the exchange.

It suited Wyndham to be obtuse this evening. He had some questions to put to Mr. Jasper Dakins. Telling Jem to wait here with the curricle, he walked the short distance with the two younger men, chatting inconsequentially.

Outside the Spotted Dog, Jasper turned mulish. "No. I'm not going in. You two hit it off so well, you don't need me. I'm done for the night."

"Now, Jas," Whistler protested, but he made no attempt to stop him. Jasper nodded curtly and took himself off into the sea-misty night.

Wyndham smiled at the disconcerted young man and nodded toward the tavern. "Shall we?" Jasper had temporarily outmaneuvered him, but perhaps his friend knew something.

The Spotted Dog was smoky and dark with paneled oak. Its benches and roughhewn tables were so deeply impregnated with the smell of ale that it tickled the nose and whetted the palate. After ordering a supper of oysters and Welsh rarebit from a melancholy barman called Pits, Crawford and the Honorable Wilfred Whistler settled down to wait with their tankards of ale.

Most of the customers were dock workers or fishermen, and their Sussex speech was so thick it was nearly incomprehensible.

"Forgive me, Whistler . . ."

"Call me Freddie."

"Freddie. Isn't the Spotted Dog rather a ramshackle place for a young buck like yourself?"

Whistler explained that it was a little rough. "Get all sorts here, and that's the truth. Even smugglers, I venture to say. But when your pockets are to let, you can't go wrong here. The food is good and the brandy is superb. Cheap, too. Stands to reason, no tax. Rotten shame Jas isn't with us, though. A lot of fun usually. Something eating him lately." The Hon. Freddie shook his head mournfully.

"Does Dakins frequent the Spotted Dog as well?"

"Why, he was the one told me about the place!"

Their conversation was interrupted by the arrival of the oysters, and for a few minutes the two were busy proving that the cook at the Spotted Dog wasn't bad at all.

After pushing back his plate and calling for a brandy, Wyndham began to probe the shallow depths of his new friend's understanding. "About Dakins. He sheered off because of me, you know. I'm a friend of the family, and he thinks I'll run home with tales of his deep doings in Brighton. The thing is, his mother's a bit worried about him."

"Why? Dropped a bundle tonight, though he was three thousand ahead once. Still and all, I don't think he's in dun country. He had a stack of Yellow Boys at the races Saturday that would have choked a horse."

"Wonder where he got them?" Wyndham asked with pretended casualness.

If Whistler knew, he didn't tell. "Won 'em, I suppose," he shrugged.

But as the Major walked the dark streets back to where Jem was waiting with the curricle, he wondered about that. Perkins had suggested something else. Yet the fact that Jasper was gambling beyond his means was no more incriminating than his frequenting a low tavern on the waterfront. That was no proof of anything but youthful extravagance and poor judgment.

Let the fool hang himself, Crawford thought impatiently. Why am I bothering? Jasper and Samantha were a well-matched pair of pea gooses. They deserved each other.

Much put out at this conclusion, the Major arrived back at the Red Lion in good time to have a word with Jelli before retiring to Lady Fitz's house for the night.

Jasper, surprisingly, was still awake, nursing a drink and a sad countenance at a table near the fire.

Wyndham approached him, not noticing the shabby stranger who had just entered the inn, and was now standing at the door of the common room.

"So we meet again, Dakins. How goes it?" Without waiting for an invitation, Major Crawford sat down beside him.

"Wonderful," Jasper answered and drained his glass.

"I suppose you know that Miss Crawford and Lady Fitzcameron are in town."

"I called on them yesterday."

"I see."

They sat silently and stared at the fire, paying no need to the newcomer who walked quietly to the bar and asked for a pint.

"You trying to finance that stud farm at the faro table?" It wasn't exactly tactful, but then tact wasn't one of the Major's virtues in any case.

"How did you guess?"

"Give it up. Faro is dangerous."

Jasper turned his head, and for the first time really looked at the slightly frowning face of his companion. "What do you mean, sir? You are involving yourself in my affairs in a way I find distasteful." His face suffused with color, and his tone was haughty, but as his eyes drifted past the Major to the man at the bar, their expression changed from peevish to frightened. "Leave me alone, Crawford."

The Major stood up. "As you say. Still, my advice to you is to give it up. I hope to see you when you are in better spirits. Good evening."

Crawford bowed slightly and strode over to say good night to Sergeant Jellison. "Well, Jelli! What did you make of that?" he asked ruefully.

"Seems the young man don't care to talk."

"Not to me, at any rate. It's a pity, too, for I mean him well. But Dakins has chosen his own road. Let's hope he doesn't come to grief over it . . . though if what I'm beginning to suspect is true, he's in trouble."

The man at the other end of the bar downed his ale quickly and walked out. The Major didn't notice the meaningful nod he exchanged with Jasper.

CHAPTER 11

While Wyndham was spending his first evening in Brighton in a very different part of town, Samantha was seated in the Draytons' elegant drawing room. Her thoughts, though, were not on the trio of wobbly sopranos gathered by the piano. Indeed, she scarcely heard any of the music presented that evening. Samantha was too bemused by the startling change in her circumstances to concentrate on the definitely limited talents of the Drayton sisters.

Lady Fitzcameron had bundled her out of the Pillars and down to Brighton before she had a chance to reconsider her promise, though Hester needn't have worried. Samantha would never go back on her word. But once settled in the pleasant house that her aunt had rented in the best part of town, Samantha began to think that she had been gammoned. Lady Fitz's spirits had recovered their usual sparkle with surprising speed, and her dire financial problems managed to right themselves after one brief visit to the ailing Mr. Maddens.

Aunt Hester had refused to allow Samantha to accompany her to the poor man's sickroom in spite of her original plea for support. It was all very suspicious, especially when Lady Fitzcameron returned from her man of business in tearing spirits, full of plans for outfitting Samantha from head to toe. It did no good to argue, because the old lady swore she had just received a windfall in unexpected revenues, and she was determined to spend it on her dear, sweet niece. When the independent Miss Crawford tried to decline her aunt's lavish gift, she was overruled immediately.

"I am here for two weeks, dear girl, and as fond as I am of you, I cannot allow you to go about looking such a dowd. I'll warrant that thing you're wearing once belonged to Bunch."

"Aunt Hester! How can you say so? It is not new, I grant you, but the seamstress in the village assured me it was the latest mode but two years ago."

"Ten years is more like it," she snorted. "I'll hear no more about it, Samantha. Either you allow me to order you a few new gowns, or you destroy my reputation forever."

Samantha finally acquiesced, but the few gowns turned out to be more in the nature of a new wardrobe. She protested that as a companion she would have little use for three ball gowns, one spun in pure silver, no less, or the dark blue velvet riding habit trimmed with ermine. But Lady Fitz paid no attention to these pragmatic arguments and continued to lavish on her wide-eyed niece every fal-lal of fashion that took her fancy.

And indeed Samantha did pay for dressing. Her excellent figure showed to perfection in the narrow, clinging gowns, and her soft blond hair, cut and curled by the great Jacques himself, now adorned her proud head like a golden crown.

Queenly was too matronly a word to describe Samantha the first time she ventured out as a lady of fashion, but there was something undoubtedly regal about her bearing that caused quite a few heads to turn. She was made self-conscious at first by all the attention that came her way but soon became quite used to the approving glances cast in her direction.

The ladies found Samantha's manners charming, and to a one, they envied her ability to wear the spencer, a short, tight jacket that was most unkind to the fuller figure.

Lady Fitzcameron and Miss Crawford were immediately invited to every home of note, and though much was due to Lady Fitz's own social standing, and a few discreet hints of Miss Crawford's immense fortune, some invitations were a tribute to Samantha herself. The gentlemen in particular found her an engaging companion, and more and more Samantha was becoming the center of attention at any gathering. She was blissfully unaware of her aunt's strategy to insure her success and never guessed that it was her imaginary bank account that warmed most hearts. In consequence, Miss Crawford was proclaimed everywhere as charmingly modest.

Lady Fitzcameron, of course, was basking in her niece's success and when they weren't receiving guests or dining out, she kept Samantha busy with fittings and shopping excursions, until the wardrobes in the small house were soon strained to their limits.

But if Hester had hopes from all of this, Samantha did not. She accepted it as an entertaining interlude and was determined not to let her uncertain future mar her enjoyment of it. This was the world denied to her when she was young, and Samantha was discovering both its delights and limitations. A sedate ride in the park was not as exciting as a morning gallop along the beach, but it had its own merit as one met and chatted with all sorts of acquaintances. The polite round of morning calls, each lasting twenty minutes by the clock, could be either yawningly long or tantalizingly short depending on the people present. Samantha would have enjoyed visiting the circulating library or the many scenic spots nearby, but her aunt kept her too busy to take time for such unimportant diversions.

The first week passed swiftly, and Samantha lived each day to the full, yet Aunt Hester was becoming increasingly restless. She had dashed off a couple of quick notes at the beginning of their stay, and then, as the days went by, took to lingering about the house until the post arrived. She would snatch up the day's arrivals, then toss them away with an exasperated groan.

Samantha refrained from asking her aunt what she was expecting in the mail, thinking it might concern the drastic reversal in her finances. But whatever it was, Lady Fitz would tell her in her own good time, Samantha reasoned. Meanwhile her days were too filled to wonder about it much. As it turned out, she was put out of her suspense rather sooner than she expected. When they returned home from the Draytons that evening, Burns informed them that Major Crawford had arrived but had gone out directly after changing his clothes.

Lady Fitzcameron was suddenly all smiles again and cried for Samantha to set out her prettiest dress for tomorrow as Wyndham would be escorting them to the theatre.

Samantha felt a spurt of pleasure at the thought that Major Crawford was bound to be impressed when he saw her in her new finery. Then she brought herself sharply to task. "Do not depend on the Major, Aunt. He may have other plans."

"Never. I wrote and explained that I required his presence in Brighton; after all, my dear, there are occasions when a gentleman does round out a party, and he has obliged, as you see. Four days late," she grumbled, "but he is here now."

Samantha ascended the stairs behind her aunt, listening with half an ear to her cheerful babbling. So the Major was the cause of her megrims. I should have known, Samantha thought with more than a touch of irony.

Lady Fitzcameron had every reason to be in sunny spirits again. Her plot was working to perfection. Wyn may not have exactly rushed to obey her imperious summons to get himself to Brighton without further delay, but he was here now, and that's what counted. He couldn't fail to be impressed by the transformation wrought in Samantha.

And indeed Hester was hard put not to laugh out loud at the expression on his face the following morning when they all met in the breakfast room.

His jaw had not precisely dropped; after all, Wyn was too seasoned a military man to allow a flank attack to disconcert him. But his abominable tongue was kind for a change, and he managed a compliment without sounding pontifical.

The fact that the Major was suitably impressed by the dash Samantha cut in a yellow sarcenet morning dress with daisies embroidered on the sleeve and the hem prompted her to return a compliment of her own. "You are very fine yourself, sir. That coat is one I have not seen before, and your cravat is most elegant. The Waterfall, is it not?"

Wyndham was quite pleased that Miss Crawford had noticed. "Holiday garb, ma'am," he grinned. "It would be a waste of effort to spend half an hour tying my neckcloth with only Doolittle and the stableboys to admire the effect. In Brighton it is a different matter, and a mere half hour and the spoiling of four freshly starched cravats is not too extreme when one considers the honor of the Crawford name."

"Only one half hour," Samantha mused with a twinkle in her eye. "My cousin Jasper tells me that it takes him nearly twice that long to achieve even moderate results."

Their glances met in shared amusement, but Lady Fitz was quick to check any unfavorable comparison that Samantha might make against Wyndham. "Hmph," she snorted. "Jasper could spend all morning getting up the dandy and still not appear nearly so well. The Crawfords were always a fine-looking family."

The Major agreed that it was certainly true of the

female portion. "Indeed, you are both so fetching that it would be to my advantage to show you off by a ride in the park. To see and be seen is one of the delightful duties of town life."

Hester was vastly pleased that her remark produced such prompt action, though she declined for herself. "You two children go. I must attend to some correspondence, and I did promise to pay a call on dear Miss Mackay. I fear you would find that sadly dull, Samantha."

"Then you will join me, Miss Crawford?" the Major asked. "If it is an added inducement, we can ride on horseback and leave the carriage for a day when the weather is less inviting. I did take the liberty of hiring some cattle while we're here. Bold Manners, a gentle mare, should do you very well. Don't let the name alarm you."

Samantha suppressed a smile. "I'd be delighted, Major. Just allow me five minutes to change into a habit."

Not only was Samantha within the allotted time, but again won the Major's admiration as she descended the stairs in a dark blue velvet riding habit and a plumed hat which sat on her head at a charming angle. He made good his word and directed their ride through the busiest section of the park, where quite a few other horsemen were taking advantage of the bright weather.

They had just completed a round, when Jasper Dakins spotted them and came prancing over on a raking black with very bad manners. It immediately attempted to nip Samantha's placid hack on the withers, and there was a flurry of shouts and dancing hooves before all three riders were in control again.

"Sorry. I've only had him a week. He's called Satan. Appropriate, ain't it?" Jasper rattled on, but Samantha noticed that he looked both tired and nervous, more nervous than a mere incident with a new horse would warrant.

"If he isn't schooled properly, it would seem only common sense to keep him away from other riders. If Miss Crawford's horse had not been such a sluggard, there might have been an accident." Wyndham looked disapprovingly at Dakins.

"Nonsense," Samantha said roundly. "Though you have no cause to know it, Major, I am an adequate horsewoman."

"Adequate? More than that," Jasper affirmed. "Samantha is a bruising rider! By the way, Sammie, meant to tell you. You're looking much more the thing since Lady Fitzcameron took you in hand. A large improvement, I'd say!"

The effrontery of that remark nettled Wyndham, but far from being displeased, Samantha was dimpling up at the insolent cub as if he had said the pretty.

"I'm glad you approve," she said, a sunny smile warming her face. "We haven't seen more of you by moving to Brighton, Jasper. You have been neglecting us. However, Major Crawford is seeing to our needs. He is escorting us to the theatre this evening." Samantha's tone was light as she was too used to the Dakins family habit of giving backhanded compliments to be other than amused at Jasper's attempt at

135

gallantry. She turned a happy face to the Major. "I must say that I find Brighton delightful. There is something of interest happening every minute. Not only music and dancing but the theatre, as well. I know that to you it is the veriest commonplace, but I am the country mouse come to town. It's all quite marvelous to me."

Major Crawford assented, delighted that the staid Miss Crawford was coming out of her shell at last. And the metamorphosis was astonishing. It wasn't only the new clothes; her very demeanor was fresh and sparkling. It appeared that Lady Fitz had succeeded, after all.

That evening at the Theatre Royale Samantha watched the performance with such palpable excitement that Wyndham found himself more taken with his engrossed companion than with Edmund Kean. The new star of the English theatre was repeating in Brighton his triumphant interpretation of Shylock. The audience was well pleased, and the applause was long and exuberant. Indeed a royal duke became so intemperate in his enthusiasm that he burst through his tight-fitting breeches and had to helped from his box.

Samantha and the Major had been watching this byplay with interest, and to Wyndham's delight Samantha again showed her roguish sense of humor.

"His pink undergarments clash dreadfully with his green waistcoat, don't you agree, Major?"

"Absolutely, Miss Crawford. No decent valet would have overlooked such a contingency."

"I agree. The Duke should either dismiss the man,

136

or, at the very least, order a dozen new coats to match his . . . ah, drawers."

Wyndham laughed appreciatively, vastly enjoying this entertaining facet of Samantha's personality. He had always suspected that under the drab feathers that covered Miss Crawford lay another creature, but the change in her was even more pronounced than he would have guessed possible. Not only had her naturally buoyant spirits surfaced, but her appearance had improved remarkably. The overly pale face that showed far too many signs of fatigue and strain now glowed rosily. Her blue eyes sparkled with excitement, and her hair, once so colorless and unbecoming, was released from the confining knot and fashionably dressed. It was only a shame that those charms were reserved for someone quite undeserving. That's what galled the Major so. While Samantha was preening herself for her irresponsible cousin, the boy showed no appreciation of her at all.

But Samantha's sky was unclouded at the moment. She was drinking in the glories of Brighton like a man denied water for too long. Surprisingly the advent of Major Crawford on the scene was an added fillip. In some ways he seemed a different person in Brighton than the rude military man she found so maddening. Not only were his manners more pleasing, but he showed a definite improvement in temper as well. Not once had he barked at her or taken her to task for some petty misdemeanor. Even his taste in clothing was far superior to the rustic garments he wore at home. The Major cut quite a dash in black evening clothes, though his preference still ran to the subdued rather than the flamboyant. What surprised her most, though, was his ease in society. Samantha would have thought that a military man might feel out of place playing the gallant, but not only was the Major adept at turning a compliment, he was experienced in court circles, too.

Samantha was suffering some apprehension about her presentation to the Prince Regent. If she had made her curtsy when most girls do, at their debut in society, she'd be a seasoned hand by now. But being at the advanced age of twenty-six before an introduction to court was causing her some anxiety. The Major lessened her trepidation by recounting his own first experience, which he assured her would put her own worries in the shade.

"I was but a raw subaltern on leave and gone to Newmarket for the races. I'd put my money on the favorite, the Prince's horse, a beautiful three-year-old bay called Jenny Come Love Me. Yes, Miss Crawford, that was the name." He chuckled to himself. "Word ran that the filly had been named for a pretty serving wench who had caught the Prince's eye at the time . . . . ." Wyndham then remembered his company and coughed slightly. "But that's all beside the point." He flashed a look at Miss Crawford, expecting her to be coldly disapproving of a tale that had begun to border on the unseemly, but she was thoroughly amused.

"Go on," she prompted. "Did Jenny Come Love Me win?"

"You are rushing to the finish line too quickly," he smiled back. "It was nip and tuck all the way. The

At home, Lady Fitzcameron complained that the reception had been a horrid squeeze and quite insufferably warm.

Samantha agreed. "Sometimes I could not move for the press of people, and such a dreadful wait we had just to get a glass of orgeat. But I am very pleased to have gone. Did you notice, Aunt, that the ceiling in the dining room was designed as an enormous palm tree?"

"Yes. Very splendid if one cares for such things," Lady Fitzcameron sniffed.

"Now why should fat little cherubs be in the best of good taste, and a palm tree vulgar?" asked Samantha innocently.

To Hester's surprise Major Crawford found a great deal to laugh about over that absurd comment.

One afternoon later that week, after returning from yet another party, Wyndham felt assured enough in his relationship with Samantha to ask, "You can't tell me that you still frown on the frivolous pursuits of society, Miss Crawford. I refuse to believe it after the way you led poor Lord Ottley around by the nose all afternoon."

"I was trying to escape his attentions, as you well know, Major. But you are right about the other. I must have sounded terribly pompous when I condemned all society out of hand. Now that I've had an opportunity to savor its delights, I fear I have become as frivolous as any other. You may laugh, Major, but though I am most grateful to Aunt Hester and wouldn't have missed this for the world, these fashionable amusements are like sweetcakes. An overindulgence could spoil the strongest stomach."

"You are a wise, young philosopher, and quite right, of course. Nevertheless, I have found these last few days only a tempting morsel. In your company, I think no pleasure could become stale."

"Why, Major Crawford," Samantha dimpled, a sparkle of mischief lighting her eyes. "Brighton has changed you out of all recognition. Here, you commend my good sense, laugh at my witticisms, and strew compliments about with prodigious extravagance. I am not quite sure it is the same man."

"Perhaps the 'frivolous pursuits of society' have amended both our manners. You did not smile at me so charmingly at home, nor have you raked me over the coals for my sins even once this sennight." His expression was light, and he bowed handsomely as if to deny any hint of reproof in his words.

Samantha accepted it as no more than the truth, though she was hard put to understand the reason for this welcome change in their relationship. From the cool politeness that had disguised tolerance, or most often irritation, they had insensibly moved to a flirtatious friendship. It couldn't be due to her new wardrobe, Samantha thought with irony. Nor could she claim that the Major's town bronze had won her over. Perhaps it was merely the effects of Brighton itself.

Amelia had explained after her first London Season that flirtations were merely all part of the game played by the *ton*. It was considered a normal courtesy to pay outrageous compliments, and the ladies accepted these gracious tributes as a sign of good manners. No one took these blandishments seriously. A girl who refined too much on a show of gallantry was either green, or openly husband hunting. Marriages were contracted on the basis of settlements and business arrangements.

Samantha chided herself for reading anything more personal in the Major's conduct than mere politeness. It was not what she wished in any case. This was but an interlude in her life, not a permanent change. She could enjoy it as a temporary diversion only.

But was Jasper being as sensible? He had been complaining for years that the income from his father's estate was a paltry sum, quite inadequate to maintain the role of leisured gentleman that he longed to play. Yet suddenly her cousin seemed flush with wealth: a new horse, some very dashing, even dandified clothes, and rumors of high stakes pledged and lost in the most fashionable gaming clubs of Brighton.

His acquaintance with Lady Fitz had given him *entrée* into the highest circles, and Samantha realized with dismay that the fashionables of the *ton* assumed he had a large fortune to back up his pretensions. Mothers with marriageable daughters were even asking discreet questions about the personable Mr. Dakins, and Samantha was in a quandary how to answer them.

When she asked Jasper how he was able to pay for his extravagances, he grinned and said that he hadn't. "Bought 'em on tick," he laughed. "Never mind, Sammie, I can pay for it all. Made a killing at the racetrack."

Samantha hoped it was true, but could one really win so much money there?

Pushing these worries aside, Samantha prepared for the grand ball that was to close her two-week stay in Brighton. The Prince Regent was giving a magnificent party at the Royal Pavilion in honor of a visiting Russian princess, and Lady Fitzcameron had wangled an invitation for the three of them.

It was rumored that the Prince had imported four hundred pounds of caviar to be served by twenty midgets in full Cossack military uniform, complete with miniature swords, but this was later discounted as a nasty Tory invention, though the dinner was lavish enough without that. Sixty sat down to dine on the Regent's gold plate while an army of servants hovered over them, offering an assortment of no less than forty dishes. The only thing that might have been called extreme was the Russian troika filled with hothouse flowers that was driven right into the dining room. Princess Sarnoff accepted the tribute graciously and solved the problem of how to transport this fragile gift halfway across Europe by presenting each lady at the table with a floral bouquet.

But it was the dancing later that Samantha was to remember most clearly. Lord Ottley claimed the first waltz, and after that she went from one partner to the next with barely a moment to rest. The musicians had begun a reel when the Major finally claimed her hand, and they whirled through the complicated steps, meeting at the end of the line. Samantha was breathless when it was over, but Wyndham requested the next dance also.

"Unless you would prefer to sit this one out?" he offered.

"Only if you will keep me company while I indulge myself with a brandied sweetmeat."

Finding two vacant seats, the Major left Samantha for a moment to procure the sweet, then returned with a plate filled with an assortment of delicacies. "I thought you might like to try this chocolate cream, too. My favorite is the cherry tart."

"We spoke of overindulgence," Samantha said between bites, "but tell me, does the Prince always serve two hundred as though they were two thousand?"

"He has been known to stint on occasion. I remember once being offered only four fish courses."

"How paltry. Well, he certainly made up for it this evening. By the way, I never did thank you properly for the horse you hired for me."

"I am ashamed, Miss Crawford. Had I the least notion you were such a fine rider, I would have chosen something more up to your weight. I am very particular about horses."

"Then that is another passion we share besides cherry tarts." She colored slightly at his curious look. "Horses, I meant."

They were about to enter the next set of dancing, when Lady Fitzcameron came out of the card room and, pleading a headache over her losses at piquet, asked to be taken home.

"You children can stay. That is, you are certainly

free to return, Wyn." She put a hand to the lavender turban on her head. "But I wish for nothing better than my hartshorn and a glass of Burgundy in the quiet of my own bedchamber."

Samantha protested at making the Major return just for her. The Prince had departed a short while ago, and most people were taking their leave. She had wanted to stay until the last moment, as this was their final evening in Brighton, but she gave only one wistful thought to another dance with the Major, then helped her aunt out to the waiting carriage. The party was over, anyway.

Samantha and Lady Fitzcameron left for home the next morning while Burns closed up the house. Explaining that business matters prevented him from returning to the Pillars with them, the Major removed himself to the Red Lion where Jellison had a room ready for him. Wyndham still hadn't had the serious talk with Jasper that he had promised himself and after what some other inquiries had revealed, he felt it prudent to do so immediately.

But alas for Major Crawford's plans. Jellison assured him regretfully that young Dakins had left for home early that morning. The rest of the day passed with irritating slowness, and when Wyndham finally found himself at Mrs. Lark's establishment, Whistler was not present. A desultory game of piquet with the proprietress was equally unrewarding, except for the lures she threw out to him. The Major wasn't sure why he refused them, but suddenly he was filled with an urge to return home.

Feeling bored and ill-used, Wyndham said good

night to his hostess and walked back through the quiet lanes to the Red Lion. It was not late yet, but rather that quiet time of night after all the good middle-class people have gone to bed, and everyone else is busy about their pleasures.

The deserted and fog-shrouded streets held no terrors for the Major. His swagger stick was a formidable deterrent to any who might think of waylaying the tall figure in the caped greatcoat. Yet the Major could not have been called alert. His mind was busy with the revelations of the last few days.

If he had asked a lot of questions, the answers had been ambiguous. There was no proof that Jasper Dakins was other than a shallow, pleasure-seeking youth, whose expensive habits belied his limited means. Yet the Major felt sure the boy was involved in mischief. How did he come to frequent a low establishment like the Spotted Dog? And what was he doing in conversation with a middle-aged sailor?

Apparently Miss Crawford shared none of his suspicions about her cousin. She positively glowed these past days, the Major thought with satisfaction. Lady Fitz had mapped her strategy well. Now that the stubborn Samantha Crawford had been shown the kind of life she should be leading, she would not be so all-fired obstinate about leaving the Pillars.

The Major was so engrossed in that speculation that he paid no heed to the faint tap of footsteps that had followed him from Mrs. Lark's. But as he was about to turn the corner to the Red Lion, the sound of running feet roused him from his revery, and he spun around instinctively.

The man behind him had a large cudgel in his hand, and he swung it at the Major's head. Wyndham ducked and at the same time struck a savage blow to the man's stomach with his swagger stick. There was a grunt of pain, and the man backed off, dropping the cudgel as he clutched at his ribs. Then he took to his heels and disappeared down a dark alley.

Wyndham stood his ground, a little dazed by the quickness of events. Only his long experience with night patrols had saved him. Consciously he had made no decisions; his fighting instincts had simply taken over. How absurd it would have been to die in an alley in Brighton after surviving the war!

Frustrated and angry, Wyndham strode the last few yards to the door of the Red Lion. The evening had been a fiasco all around. He should have gone home with the ladies and saved himself a load of trouble.

CHAPTER 12

It was just past four the next afternoon when the Major returned to the Pillars. The ladies were about to pour tea when he strode in, by now in a fair state of controlled anger.

He tossed his riding cape to Perkins, then loaded a plate with sandwiches, refusing a cup of freshly brewed tea in favor of a tankard of ale.

Lady Fitzcameron looked at Wyndham's ill-tempered face and chuckled. "What's eating you, boy? Did you swallow a lemon?"

The Major forced a grimace that might pass for a smile and asked rather curtly where he might find Captain Trumbull. Samantha informed him that Stacey had ridden over to Dakins Hall to call on Elizabeth this afternoon.

"He will be back for dinner," she said at the Major's expression of impatient dismay.

Wyndham finished his sandwiches in moody silence and excused himself shortly after, leaving both ladies to speculate on what could have occurred since they left him in Brighton. Something had put him seriously out of spirits.

"Business," opined Lady Fitz wisely. "Never mind. He's not one to sulk long."

Stacey returned from Dakins Hall that evening with four handwritten invitations. A birthday ball was planned for Amelia this sennight, and everyone at the Pillars was entreated to attend. The news was greeted with varying shades of interest and delight, Stacey being the most euphoric. Hester wasn't far behind. How ravishing Samantha would look in the silver ball gown with the Fitzcameron diamonds at her throat! She would quite outshine Amelia for a change. And with her golden hair in the Grecian mode . . . why, all the other girls would be cast in the shade.

While the two women discussed the projected ball in absorbing detail, Wyndham steered his friend into the library. Once closeted within, he described last evening's assault.

"A footpad," Stacey nodded.

"That's what I thought at first, but there are some facts that have me concerned." Wyndham was pacing up and down the gloomy chamber, a worried frown on his face. "For instance, such attacks are far more common down near the waterfront. I was at the Red Lion, and that's a decent neighborhood. Nor was I drunk. No one could have thought me an easy mark."

"These cutthroats have grown bold. There are desperate men about since the peace. Discharged soldiers with no future prospects are hungry enough to try anything. They say it is not safe to walk on many a London street," Stacey observed.

Wyndham shook his head. "But Brighton is not London, and the pickings are leaner in a smaller town. I'll lay odds that the fellow was a sailor and not ill-fed, by the weight of him."

"What did he look like? If you saw him, you should lay a charge against him with the magistrate."

"That I did, and it took the better part of two hours, as well as being the most futile occupation I ever attempted. My patience has been sore tried, Stace. And all because I was concerned for Jasper Dakins."

Captain Trumbull gave his friend a grim smile. "I see where you are leading. Best tell me all, Wyn."

The Major ran his fingers through his thick hair and began pacing the room. "It may be that I am starting at shadows, but one of my reasons for going to Brighton was to find out more about Dakins's activities. All I've gotten are some smoky answers, yet they are disturbing in themselves." He went on to explain that his curiosity was first aroused when Jasper openly approved of free trading, then denied that it was practiced around here. After that, Dakins came to the Major for a loan, which he refused, but turned up in Brighton shortly following, unaccountably plump in the pocket. Wyndham asked a few discreet questions about Jasper's apparent prosperity and was set upon in a dark street.

Captain Trumbull let out a low whistle. "A case of curiosity killing the cat, eh?"

"But why?" Wyndham asked. "What can he gain even if he is behind it?"

"Your silence, for one thing. If Dakins is tied in with the smugglers, he'd be very uncomfortable about your open declaration to stop them. Most of the locals, even landowners, turn a blind eye to what's going on right under their noses. They all profit by it one way or another, even if it is only a keg of brandy. Now you arrive on the scene, kick up a fuss, and go so far as to talk to the preventives about it. It seems the 'gentlemen' don't like that, Wyn. You've been told to stop. Remember, my friend, murder has been done before to protect their illicit trade."

"If they meant to kill me, they are a paltry crew. I haven't a mark on me. It's the other fellow who's nursing bruises today."

"Oh, I know you're a tough nut, but I recommend that you take care. This business is nastier than you may think."

Stacey's prophecy proved to be only too true. In the next morning's post a note came for Wyndham, obviously slipped in with the regular mail. The envelope was addressed in a crude hand to 'Squire Crawford, the Pillars.' Inside was a message, brief, but confirming Wyn's conjectures.

YOU HAVE BEEN WARNED. KEEP YOUR NOSE OUT OF WHAT AIN'T YOUR BUSINESS.

The morning was well advanced by the time the Major arrived at the old manor, and the sun was playing hide-and-seek behind thick, gray clouds that seemed to promise rain. Tethering Lady securely on the sea side of the house, he began a systematic search.

His polished boots were soon marked and muddy as he quartered back and forth along the steep hillside, but at no point was there any indication that a pathway had once been cleared to descend from the edge of the cliff down to the beach. Rather than break down the front door of the manor and look through a maze of rooms to find a secret passageway, the Major decided there was nought to do but look for the tunnel from the beach. Bracing himself against the steep angle, he clambered down the slope, arriving at the bottom in a shower of stones and bracken.

He walked along the narrow strip of sand, scanning every irregularity in the side of the hill, when he noticed two boulders of almost identical size and shape, sitting side by side. Wondering if such similarity were an artifice of nature or a man-made formation, he came closer to inspect the oddity. As he thought, one large stone sat slightly in front of the other so a sizable opening lay between them. Feeling around with his hands first, the Major made a cautious entry, and as his eyes adjusted to the gloom, he made an interested appraisal.

The ceiling was only only inches from the top of his head, and it was buttressed with rough beams. The walls curved inward from the weight of the mountain overhead, and the dirt floor was damp from moisture. The tunnel had not been abandoned, though. Next to him, in a niche, was a crude shelf holding a lantern and a store of candles.

Striking a light and fixing a candle in the holder, the Major headed up the steeply sloping passageway, giving only brief thought to the danger of meeting some member of the smugglers' gang. They must use it at night, he reasoned, and shun the place in the light of day.

The tunnel narrowed and grew steeper as it climbed higher inside the hill, and the Major found his ears straining to hear something in the oppressive silence. But the only countervail to the weighty quiet was the thudding of his own heart and the distant beat of waves on the shore. The lantern threw a circle of light that in itself was comforting, but outside its ring was a stygian gloom never encountered under the blessed sky, no matter how dark. This burrowing beneath the ground was unnerving, and Wyndham had to shake off a sense of unease.

As he proceeded cautiously, his light casting grotesque shadows on the decaying beams overhead, he noticed that further along the passage there was a divergence in the shape of the tunnel. The wall appeared to jut out at an angle. Then the Major saw that it was a thick, nail-studded door hinged into a wooden frame.

His approach was cautious, but when he heard nothing from within, he opened the door and shone his lamp about. The stone-lined room was empty; no casks or boxes to explain the faint outline of footprints on the dirt floor. It was obviously a secret room built for storage. The watertight walls proved that. As the Major was about to withdraw, he heard the distinct sound of footsteps in the passageway outside. Closing the door and shielding the light with a fold of his coat, he darted into a corner.

The door creaked slightly as it was pushed open, and a cloaked and hooded figure, holding a dripping candle, entered with hesitant steps.

The Major spoke up sharply. "Turn around slowly. I have a cocked pistol in my hand."

The figure let out a choked cry and dropped the candle, then tried to jump back through the open door. Immediately Wyndham grabbed a handful of woolen cloak.

"Who are you?" he demanded, raising the lantern to better see his captive's face. Candlelight gleamed on golden hair and wide, frightened eyes.

"Miss Crawford!"

Samantha reeled under the Major's accusing gaze, and for a moment wondered if he would indeed use the pistol on her. Her clever notion of this morning now seemed the very height of folly.

It was concern that had sent Samantha to the old manor, armed with only a flint and candle, and a growing apprehension that the derelict ruin truly might be a rendezvous for the smugglers. From what she had seen in Brighton, it was not so impossible to believe that Jasper had made good his threat to turn to crime, and if so, it was also likely that he would be tempted to make use of his knowledge of the tunnel. If Major Crawford had not become as irascible as he was before their trip to Brighton, she might have voiced her suspicions to him. But their truce was too tenuous to risk breaking it so soon. Now that the reality of being home once more was upon them, Samantha decided it was wiser to keep her own counsel.

After letting herself into the manor with a massive key—a duplicate of the one she had turned over to the Major—Samantha made her way through the empty rooms and down the steep, black oak stairs to the cellars. By the time she got to the cobwebbed door that led to the tunnel, she was covered with dust herself and no closer to discovering any evidence that the house was being used by smugglers. But gazing up at the owner of the decaying grandeur that silently surrounded them, Samantha's fears returned. It appeared that the Major had come across more than cobwebs.

For a moment they were breast to breast, and Samantha was as aware of the masculine strength that upheld her as the Major was of her terrified heart. He quickly released his hold on her cape.

Pulling herself together with an effort, she attempted to regain her composure. "Major Crawford," she said, bravely lifting her face to examine his shadowed features. "How you frightened me."

He did not appear to be contrite. "Did I? What if you had encountered one of the notorious smugglers? Would he have frightened you as much?"

"Why, no . . . of course. I was not expecting to find anyone here." Her heart began to pound with a different kind of fear as he raked her with a harsh scrutiny that left her weak at the knees.

"Then what brings you here, Miss Crawford? Curiosity?"

"Of course." To escape those probing eyes, Samantha scanned the gloomy depths of the room. Surprisingly her voice was quite in control when she spoke. "The games we played here. I often pretended to be a pirate with a knife in my hand, ready to fight for a treasure of Spanish doubloons."

"Then it was you who marked this lantern as your own."

In his hands was the very same sailors' lamp that Samantha had purloined from the attics when she was a child. The mark to which the Major referred was a crude skull and crossbones that Jasper had carved on it with a childish hand to show ownership.

"Where did you find this, Major? I thought the lantern was lost. It was only a plaything."

"Yet it is not so long since others played with it. The lantern was set conveniently by the entrance along with candles and flint. It certainly shows no sign of many years neglect. In fact, I'd wager it wasn't used longer than two weeks ago."

"But that's not possible. No one comes here anymore."

"Then what prompted you to make a visit, Miss Crawford? A nostalgic pilgrimage?"

"Of course not," Samantha sighed. "I had the same thought as you, Major. But I wonder if we both aren't jumping to conclusions."

"Then we are only one jump ahead of the preventive officers. Lieutenant Travers is no fool, Miss Crawford, and the same rumors that came to our

157

notice will make their way to him before long. Riding officers have many informants."

"Such as the master of the Pillars?" she challenged.

"I'm no informer, no matter what you may believe, but it behooves me to know exactly what is happening on Crawford land. There are also certain loyalties to His Majesty to consider."

"So even though you resigned your commission, you still consider yourself in the King's employ."

"No more so than any other citizen."

"We found no real evidence of smuggling, just an old lantern." She argued more to herself than the Major.

"Then you have no objection if I keep it."

"Keep it?" Samantha looked at him suspiciously. "For what reason?"

"For your peace of mind, Miss Crawford. After all, it is your property."

"Not any more, it appears. Just throw it away, Major. Destroy it. I never want to see it again."

Wyndham had been playing the inquisitor up to now, but the desperate appeal in Samantha's eyes gave him pause. Of course, she had hoped to remove any incriminating evidence that might point to Dakins. That was the purpose of her visit. And if the Major hadn't been goaded into action by that letter this morning, she might have succeeded. He could certainly understand her fear for Jasper. Aside from their close relationship, she was in love with the wretch. But this was no childhood game. The free traders were playing for high stakes, and Dakins knew the danger he ran. So did Wyndham. He couldn't overlook an attempt on his life just to appease Samantha's fears for her cousin, but he also didn't want to add to her distress by telling her about the footpad in Brighton. How could the girl be such a fool? Jasper didn't deserve her consideration, and the thought of how far she would go to protect him was infuriating to the Major. He himself had saved many a young soldier from the consequences of such folly, but destroying King's evidence was something else entirely.

With a muttered oath, the Major took her arm. "Do not deceive yourself, Miss Crawford. It is only a matter of time before the smugglers are caught, and your addlepated cousin with them."

"Please say nothing of this, Major, I beg of you. Toss away the lantern. Pretend you've never seen it."

"How can I? That would be compounding this felony."

"But you have no proof, just a suspicion."

"Which you seem to share, Miss Crawford."

Samantha could not deny that, and she turned away with a sigh. Major Crawford would not keep silent on her account, and never on Jasper's. He had taken an aversion to the boy and could not be persuaded to help him. Wyndham Crawford had an implacable sense of duty and no particular reason to bend it for people who had shown him little civility. The lighthearted man she had glimpsed in Brighton was a cold stranger again. Samantha led the way up from the cellars through the dusty reaches of the manor house kitchens to the outside.

"Quite straightforward, after all," the Major remarked curtly as they reached the front door. "No secret passages behind paneled walls, just a dank room in the cellars and a muddy tunnel to the sea."

"Were you expecting a ghost?" Samantha asked with only a hint of anger in her well-controlled voice.

"It wouldn't surprise me to find one of the ignoble Crawfords still hanging about."

"No, Major. I am the only miscreant left."

They glared at each other in a conflict of emotions. If Samantha had thought it would do any good, she would have flung herself at the Major's feet and begged him to help his people. But he had no feeling for them, unlike Samantha who knew and loved them. The Major was incapable of compassion, so she might as well save her breath.

Wyndham Crawford knew the thoughts that flitted through her mind; they were clearly written on her face. Cursing himself for a fool, he tried to allay her fears.

"I'll do nothing for the present, but that does not mean smuggling will go unpunished on my land. Yes, my land, Miss Crawford. Not your grandfather's anymore. So limit your interference to warning your friends. I will not tolerate free trading."

As usual Samantha heard the sting in his words, not the measure of them. While the Major thought he was making a concession on her behalf, Samantha thought he was issuing a threat.

"There is no need to wave your saber at me, Major, I understand you very well."

160

He gave her a long look. "I doubt that you do, my girl."

Samantha tightened her lips and jumped onto Pegasus's back without another word. What really stung was not so much the Major's threat to do his worst if his people didn't obey him, but his sharp reminder that Samantha did not belong here any longer. If for a moment she had toyed with the notion of what it would be like to stay at the Pillars under the Major's protection, it was now out of the question. The gallant attention he had paid her in Brighton was merely a sham . . . acted out under Lady Fitzcameron's orders, of course. Today he had shown his true sentiments. The Major felt no regard for the distant cousin who had been thrust on him. He would carry out his unwelcome duty toward her, but only if she did not interfere in his life. Samantha tried to work up an appropriate indignation, but she only succeeded in raising a very uncomfortable lump in her throat.

CHAPTER 13

Samantha stood still as Bunch fussed with the elaborate flounces that scalloped the hem of the silver ball gown. Its sheer silk was almost transparent, and the lace that lightly fell over the shoulder only emphasized rather than covered its daringly low-cut bodice.

Lady Fitzcameron stood by watching with an air of critical detachment. "It's actually much better than I remembered," she commented with a nod of approval. "Bunch, adjust that left sleeve . . . Ah, that's more like it."

"Happen she might fall out of it," the nurse grumbled, but her eyes shone with pleasure.

The lace demitrain was draped over Samantha's arm, adding a touch of restrained elegance, and Jenny secured a diamond butterfly in her fair curls. Lady Fitz had insisted that Samantha borrow the jeweled hairpiece for the evening as the girl foolishly refused to wear the Fitzcameron diamonds around her throat. It was little enough but perhaps the right touch after all. The smooth column of her graceful neck needed no adornment.

Gazing at her own reflection in the full-length mirror, Samantha could not push down a little thrill of pride. Who would have believed that clothes could make such a difference? The person who looked back at her with such a happy smile was not plain at all. Brighton had taught her that much, at least. Jenny exclaimed rapturously to nurse Bunch that Miss Samantha had worn that dress at Lady Kinnseyton's ball, and Bunch dabbed at her eyes and remarked that the girl put her in mind of her dear mother.

Wrapping the black velvet mantle around Samantha's shoulders, Bunch followed the two ladies as they swept down the stairs and out the front door into the waiting carriage. As it clattered away down the drive, the old nurse gave Jenny an impulsive hug.

"Can you believe it's our dear girl glowing like that? A real lady she looks."

"You should have seen her in Brighton, Miss Bunch. Why the gentlemen nearly fell over themselves to catch a glimpse of her."

"Lady Fitz was right. What the child needed was a change. And a change for the better I never did see like it."

"The master were different in Brighton, too," Jenny confessed.

"Perhaps tonight he'll ask her to marry him," Bunch sighed, her face shining with hope.

But Jenny refrained from answering. According to Jem, there were some fearful goings-on in Brighton after Miss Sam left, and the Major wasn't too happy right now. But mayhap when he saw her looking so beautiful tonight, he'd forget all about his troubles.

And what better place than a fancy party to put him in spirits again?

Dakins Hall was in *fête*. Potted flowers and palms decorated the two connecting drawing rooms that had been thrown open to accommodate the dancing, and though it was just past twilight, scores of candles made the house gleam with light.

The party from the Pillars had been invited to come early for dinner and spend the night if they wished. But Lady Fitzcameron declared she would rather drive home at four in the morning than spend any more time than necessary under the same roof as Anne Dakins. Her conversation at breakfast was enough to sour milk.

As they stood in the grand foyer to welcome their guests, the Dakins family made a handsome picture. Elizabeth was wearing sky blue, trimmed with white lace, while Mrs. Dakins's fragile prettiness was given consequence by a garnet-colored gown of shot silk. Jasper and Amelia were even more striking as they had inherited their father's dark looks, and Amelia's sultry complexion was displayed to advantage in a topaz taffeta creation that left little to the imagination.

But when the butler took the guests' wraps, it was Samantha who occasioned openmouthed admiration. Elizabeth was the first to recover, and her exclamations of delight over the silver ball gown covered the others' silence. Anne took a moment or two, then she seconded her daughter's praise, marveling to herself how two short weeks in Brighton had turned a drab moth into a glittering butterfly, like the one in Samantha's hair, she noted enviously.

Amelia only smiled slightly, then turned her attention to Wyndham. It was not the first time he had seen Samantha's gown, but he was struck again at how it flattered its wearer. Miss Dakins's dark beauty seemed almost theatrical by comparison as she smiled up at him, but he managed a compliment for her, nonetheless.

"Sammie, you're beautiful," Jasper said simply and gave her his arm.

Dinner was concluded swiftly as no one wanted to be late to receive the company, and by eight, the covers were cleared to allow the ladies time to freshen their toilette.

The musicians were just striking up when Samantha emerged from one of the guest rooms, and she was suddenly shy of appearing in public in all of her new finery. In Brighton, among strangers, she had had no such apprehensions, but she felt a little hesitant about subjecting herself to the curious eyes of those who had known her before.

Samantha was also apprehensive of Major Crawford's reaction. They had spoken scarcely a word since their encounter at the old manor, and the issue of the smugglers stood between them more sharply than ever. But they could not show their differences in public. Whatever animosity they felt for each other must be discreetly hidden by a show of friendliness. Sympathy for Samantha was growing as word of her grandfather's disposition of his property spread. If she gave a cold shoulder to the Major, it would fuel speculation that he was playing her unfair, and Samantha could not allow that rumor to persist. After all, no one would believe that Miss Crawford was leaving the Pillars voluntarily, and the new heir would find it hard going if his neighbors cast him in the role of a villain. Let them quarrel with him over his stand on the smugglers, but not for evicting the now impoverished heiress.

But Samantha need not have feared for the Major's reception. He was surrounded by a host of lovelies when she entered the ballroom, and once Jasper swept her onto the dance floor, her head rang with compliments on her gown, her looks, and the Major's generosity for setting her up in such style. That fiction was Hester's.

The company was large for a country party. At least thirty couples stood up to dance while an equal number congregated in the anterooms for whist and loo. It was a most lavish celebration for Miss Amelia Dakins's birthday, although the object of all this festivity was less than happy about the way her mousy cousin was contriving to steal the limelight. Resentment fairly glittered in Amelia's eyes as she maneuvered Samantha away from the laughing group that surrounded her.

"La, gentlemen, please. My dear cousin is not used to our society. Why, the poor girl hasn't had a chance to sit out even one dance. She needs a little ratafia to revive her." With that, Amelia then led her unwelcome burden directly over to Mrs. Dakins and deposited her in a chair under the palms. "Samantha

166

was complaining that she hasn't spoken to you all evening, Mama."

"Oh? How nice. I shall enjoy a pleasant chat."

Understanding what her cousin was about, Samantha felt it would be wise to stay put for a time. Meanwhile Mrs. Dakins was peering at her short-sightedly.

"I must admit, my dear, that I've never seen you in better looks. A little flushed now, to be sure, but then I suppose that's why you wanted a bit of a rest." Using her lorgnette, she gave Samantha's dress a careful scrutiny. "You owe a great deal to Lady Fitzcameron. I hope you are properly grateful. She needn't have done a thing for you."

As always, Mrs. Dakins's words carried a sting, but Samantha was used to such treatment. Besides, she was well aware that her own gown was casting Amelia's in the shade and that neither mother nor daughter was happy about it. Samantha had to admit to a glow of satisfaction at that. The Dakinses had pitied and mocked her deficiencies of dress so often that Samantha felt turnabout was only fair for once.

"Yes, Aunt," she answered docilely.

The lecture might have gone on for some time, but Samantha was rescued by the appearance of a tall, gangly youth who came to claim her as his promised partner in the quadrille. Looking into the tiny gold card that dangled from her wrist, Samantha agreed that this dance did indeed belong to Viscount Carrington. Making her excuses to her aunt, she whirled off on the young man's arm.

"I say," he began a bit breathlessly, flustered at

holding such an enchanting creature in his arms, "do you remember riding to the hounds with me about four seasons ago?"

"Of course, I remember. But I've given up hunting," Samantha said regretfully, giving the Viscount, who was hunting mad, the opportunity to condole with her in heartfelt sympathy.

It had been many years since Phineas had taken advantage of his neighbors' society, and old friends were gratified to see Samantha out and about again. There was talk that the old curmudgeon had lost his fortune before he died, although judging by the way his granddaughter was dressed, the Major had made up for that deficit nicely. As for Mrs. Dakins's insinuations that Miss Crawford was leaving the Pillars to become a governess, why it had to be a hum, especially since Lady Fitzcameron had hinted that Major Crawford was quite taken with the girl. A situation to bear watching, the vicar's wife told Mrs. Mainwaring.

Wyndham was just coming out of the card room when he noticed Samantha struggling through a conversation with the absentminded Squire Mainwaring. Obeying a prod from his wife, the gentleman had initialed Miss Crawford's program, but by the time his turn came to partner her, he had forgotten what it was that his spouse wanted him to ask. Relieved that he needn't trouble himself over Hetty's insatiable curiosity, he then chose to sit out the lively fling and indulge in one of his rambling monologues. This one was on the virtues of his new breed of cattle.

Samantha accepted the Major's arm with every

indication of delight when he requested the next dance. It was no doubt a duty they both would have preferred to forgo, but Samantha was determined to avoid stirring up gossip.

"I'm very glad to have an opportunity to speak to you, Major. We've hardly had a chance to discuss the outcome of our last conversation. I dared not mention it at the Pillars."

"Naturally. The only time we can manage to be civil to each other is when we are sharing one of our mutual passions," he said with an ironic twist of his mouth.

Samantha forgot her vow to smile. "I, at least, have been perfectly civil, sir," she said frostily.

"I see I have offended you again. I warned you I am no hand at gallantry."

"You seem to be having no trouble with Netty Borington."

"Is that the girl in red? Nonsensical creature. She kept telling me that my scar is romantic."

"Shameless flirt."

"I agree. A battle-scarred veteran like myself cannot hold much appeal for a young girl," the Major assented.

Samantha looked up quickly. "I did not mean that."

"Of course not. You are much too polite to call notice to my disfigurement."

Samantha was about to protest that the scar was no disfigurement when the dance ended and Jasper begged a private word with her. Wyndham bowed stiffly and left her gazing after him with a pang of regret that their conversation had been cut off so abruptly. But Jasper was already hurrying her to the library.

Quite unlike the cheerless room at the Pillars, the library at Dakins hall was all cozy warmth and inviting comfort. Samantha sank into a wing-back chair and lifted her tired feet to the warming blaze in the fireplace while Jasper took a stance by the hearth.

"Pretty dull party after Brighton, isn't it?" he asked.

"No. It's lovely. You must think me a veritable pleasure-seeker. Two weeks in Brighton out of a lifetime isn't much!"

"Poor Sam! A taste of society and then home again. I know how you feel, trapped in the country."

"You may feel that way. I don't. The country has its pleasures, too. But I thought you wanted nothing more than to bury yourself in the wilds of County Clare and raise horses. I see now that it would never do for you to be far from the delights of the city."

"That's different. I'd have something to do there. And some hope for a decent income . . ."

Samantha roused up at that. Perhaps this wasn't the best time to ask, but it was an opening she couldn't let pass.

"Jasper, where did you get the money you were spending so freely in Brighton?"

"I told you. I was lucky at the tables."

"Oh, not the races?"

"There, too."

"Then why didn't you save it to give to O'Leary?"

"O'Toole," he corrected automatically. "It's none

170

of your business, Sammie, but since you asked, it wasn't enough, not nearly enough. There wasn't any point in saving it."

Samantha shook her head at him. He was so spoiled, so childish. It was a pity, really. And she didn't believe the story of a run of luck either. "I understand you only too well, Jasper. You're making a terrible mistake if you are dealing with the free traders."

"Free traders? What makes you think I'm involved in that business?" He tried to pass it off with a laugh, but his eyes were wary.

"I was at the tunnel," Samantha told him, "and I found our lantern . . . the one with a pirate's crest on it. It's been used, Jasper, and very recently."

"Caught me out, did you?" he shrugged. "So what? All you have to do is keep your mouth shut."

Samantha was silent in consternation. She'd wanted to keep the Major out of the discussion, but now it seemed she couldn't. "Jasper, please," she implored. "It's not a game you're playing. It's your life! Major Crawford holds smuggling in little favor. If he found out . . ."

"If he found out! You wouldn't tell him, would you?"

"I think he suspects," Samantha muttered cravenly, hoping desperately that the Major hadn't said anything about it. "He was at the tunnel, too," she burst out unhappily.

With an oath Jasper whirled from her and strode the length of the room, then turned back and caught

171

her shoulders. "Tell me everything. How much does he know? Has he gone to Travers yet?"

"Let me go, Jasper."

He released her and sank to the floor at her feet, burying his head in her lap. "God! You've got to help me, Sammie! Tell me, so at least I may flee the country!"

"No. You needn't run away. I don't think he will inform the preventive officer . . . Travers, is that his name?"

"Oh, sweet Coz! I knew I could rely on you. You made him promise! How clever of you!"

"He allowed me a chance to warn you, but he won't keep silent forever. Just quit now, and there's no harm."

"I can't stop now. The next run is a big one, and my share . . ."

"Never mind about your share. It's too dangerous."

"Forget it. I'm in over my head. I thought a few runs would give me a start, enough money to get me away from here. But there are people to be paid, mouths to buy shut. Whatever I had left didn't seem to amount to very much. Oh, for the poor blokes who only need to buy a sack of barley, it's fine. But, Sammie, I need five thousand pounds."

"I suppose that's why you gambled with it, hoping to turn your share into a pot of gold. Oh, Jasper, you are a fool."

He looked very young and vulnerable suddenly. "I'm all kinds of fool, but don't worry, sweet Coz, I won't be caught in that tunnel, I promise you."

172

"Then you mean to go on with it?"

"Only one more time. I swear it, Sammie."

She put her hand to his cheek as though she would comfort a child, and Jasper placed a grateful kiss on her palm.

"You are the best girl in the world, and I am eternally in your debt. It's beyond belief that you made Crawford promise silence. Just continue to keep him quiet, and all may be well yet."

"Jasper, do not rely on that, please. I am not in the Major's confidence. If he finds out, there is no telling what he will do."

"Then it's up to you to gain that confidence. It shouldn't be too difficult. The gentleman seems to have a soft spot for you, Sammie. Just tell him I've given up my evil ways, and he'll believe you. Don't worry. With your help and a little from the gods, Crawford will never suspect a thing. And if that don't work, we'll try something else."

Samantha was about to protest this proposed collusion on her part, but a sound from the doorway made her look up. Jasper followed her gaze and jumped quickly to his feet.

"Major Crawford."

"Mr. Dakins."

"I was just leaving. Sammie and I have finished our talk. She's all yours now." With that he gave a twisted smile and took his leave.

Wyndham Crawford watched Samantha with cold eyes as she got up from the chair and walked over to him. It seemed that he had heard much of the conversation.

"Before you jump to some false conclusion, let me explain," Samantha said with a calm assumption of innocence that irritated him.

"By all means. Is this a new story, or the same fairy tale you wanted to tell me before our dance ended so inopportunely?"

Samantha clenched her hands at her sides in an attempt to remain calm. "I have never lied to you, Major."

"No. Just evaded the truth."

"How dare you . . ."

"How dare I, Miss Crawford? When all you've done for weeks is cover up for your cousin? When every honest effort I've made to try and put the estate back on its feet has met with your disapproval? I hoped that Lady Fitzcameron's influence would soften your attitude, but I see that your resentment is implacable. It's not enough that I offer you a home at the Pillars. You would rather make a monster of me by choosing a life of drudgery. Now you plot with your cousin to trick me into compliance with his illegal activities. And you ask, how dare I?"

Samantha was stunned by the Major's attack. Some of it was true, she had to admit, but the purity of her motives was never in question. Nor her honesty.

"That is unfair, Major. My only concern has been for the Pillars. I never meant to undermine your authority."

"But you have, and far beyond your fondest expectations."

"I suppose that is why you eavesdropped on a

private conversation?" she said coldly. "To catch me out in an act of perfidy against you?"

"I was not spying on you, Miss Crawford. Lady Fitzcameron sent me to summon you to her. But it seems my arrival was propitious after all. You cannot hope to deceive me now."

At that, Samantha's control snapped. Her heaving bosom could no longer contain her fury, and she lashed out at Major Crawford with the force of a lifetime's unleashed emotions.

"You are the most despicable man I have ever had the misfortune to meet. Everyone correctly took your measure when you came to the Pillars, barking orders and commands as though we were all dirt under your feet. Is it any wonder the tenants came to me with their problems? Their new master showed no touch of human compassion for their troubles. As for plotting against you, that is simply a lie. The most I have done is try to convince you that people who have always depended on the Crawfords should not be left to the tender mercies of the excisemen. But you know nothing of loyalty or love. All you know is that riding roughshod over people will cow them into submission. You are a brute, Major Crawford. A cold, unfeeling, opinionated brute."

Samantha's face was white with rage, and Wyndham's was frozen in a mask of fury. He took a menacing step closer to her, and she raised her hand to ward him off.

"I would advise you not to strike me, Miss Crawford, although now that the ladylike facade is finally down, you might discover the Crawford temper cannot be held in check so easily."

Goaded into proving him right, Samantha swung her arm and hit him in the face with all her might.

"You vixen!" the Major roared and pounced on her. His mouth assailed hers in a punishing kiss that robbed her of all resistance. She was breathless from the intensity of his anger, and shocked at her own startling response. Samantha wanted to strike at him, to pound her fists against his shoulders, but she was held captive by his strong arms and a perverse desire to submit to the onslaught of his lips.

After what seemed an eternity, his hold slackened, and he raised burning eyes to gaze into her shocked face. "I warned you," he said raggedly.

Samantha's voice came out in a harsh whisper. "You are vile."

He released her completely and stood back. "That may be, Miss Crawford. But I am not a dupe."

CHAPTER 14

Lady Fitzcameron was understandably perplexed at the turn of events. The night of the ball was to have seen the fulfillment of her plans, but something had gone miserably awry, that much was clear. Hester watched as Wyndham left the ballroom in search of Samantha and noted with dismay that he returned alone, his face grim and set. Samantha reappeared several minutes later with a blunt demand to be taken home at once. Bitterly disappointed, the old crosspatch tried to question her niece then and there and relented only when the stony looks she got in return threatened to spill over into tears. Wyn was equally unforthcoming and said he would ride home later with Captain Trumbull. Hester could get not another word out of either of them.

Samantha would always remember that evening as a nightmare. Jasper's revelations had confirmed her worst fears, but the shattering scene with the Major was just too much to be borne.

Humiliation was at the core of most of her anger, that she could have, even momentarily, been a victim of her own responses, to stand submissively while he comandeered her person. It was the surprise of his attack, she told herself, that rendered her incapable of resisting his advances. Samantha effectively blotted out her own indefensible reaction by heaping abuse upon the Major. His treatment of her was an outrage. He was a barbarian, a blackguard. How dare he listen in on a private conversation, then put his own distorted interpretation on it! Samantha had not agreed to do anything dishonorable; Jasper wouldn't ask it, she reasoned with disputable conviction. In any case the Major deserved no loyalty . . . a man of such uncompromising arrogance. If he went on his knees to her, she would never forgive him.

Samantha's only pang of conscience was at striking him. It had been wrong of her, but he had provoked her into it. Never had she felt such overpowering anger. It was his fault that she had sunk to such a vulgar display of temper. But it would never happen again; she would see to that. Samantha was no longer deluded by the Major and his false show of courtesy. If he were irritated by her displeasure before, he would shrivel under her contempt now. Yes, Wyndham Crawford was going to pay for ravaging her as though she were a conquest of war. And let the world think the worst of him.

The atmosphere at the Pillars was now heavy with discontent. Perkins snapped at Robert for every clumsy move; Hester's maid had Jenny press her mistress's gray silk four times before she was satisfied; and the Major and Samantha were successfully maintaining a wall of silence between them.

Samantha had taught him the advantage of such tactics, and now he was every bit as annoying to his antagonist as she was to him.

For two days Samantha had dinner in her room, while Stacey tried to pretend that the somber mood of his host was merely concern for the estate. There was no doubt that the Pillars was in dire straits, and its future hung precariously in the balance. But Captain Trumbull had returned from Kent with good news, and tomorrow he and the Major were going to put it to the test. Still a trip to the quarry wasn't making Wyn drink more than was his custom or snap at poor Robert when the boy forgot to refill his glass immediately. His mood could be laid at the closed door of Miss Crawford's room.

Nevertheless Major Crawford was ready early the next morning for a final inspection of the abandoned quarry. Stacey was armed with diagrams and surveying instruments, and they rode out as the sun was making its ascent over the eastern ridge.

For hours they dug and prodded, measured and aligned. At twelve they stopped to partake of the cold luncheon Cook had packed for them, and after a warming bottle of wine; began their work again. It was late afternoon by the time they got to the worn pulley system lying in pieces at the bottom of the quarry. The wood in the beams was rotted and past any practical use.

"It's got to come out," Stacey said.

"We could dismantle it, I suppose. Perhaps some of it is still usable." Wyndham kicked a fallen crossbeam.

The sun had moved to the western side of the hill, throwing a long shadow over the two men as they stood together, discussing the various possibilities. An unseen figure loomed at the top of the ridge for an instant, his shadow briefly blending with those below.

Stacey looked up absently, barely registering the slight movement, and commented that as the sun was sinking rapidly, they ought to be going. He moved a few feet away to gather up some papers he had left on the ground while Wyndham bent over to inspect the rotting beam.

The Major probed at it again with his boot, dislodging a few loose pebbles as he balanced himself against the steep side of the quarry wall. It was Stacey's sharp cry that alerted him to danger, and he looked up to see a growing avalanche descending from above.

Wyndham leaped aside and flattened himself against the cliff as a hurtling fury of stones, boulders, and dirt rained down. The noise was deafening, and it seemed an eternity before the thunder of the rockslide finally subsided. The main path of the fall had sent the larger stones cascading away from the spot where Wyndham crouched, but many of the smaller ones had showered over him with alarming force.

Stacey stumbled frantically over the loose debris to get to his friend and, with a strength born of fear, scooped away the gravel and chalk stones that buried the Major to his knees. Wyndham himself seemed dazed, and his scalp was bleeding profusely from a cut above his ear, but it soon became apparent that his right leg had suffered most. A deep gash in his thigh was already staining the ragged remnants of his breeches, and the ominous red made Stacey suck in his breath in consternation.

"You can't ride in this condition, Wyn. I'll go for help."

"Tie it up and be done, will you? I'll ride. I don't fancy lying here in the dark while my leg stiffens up."

The Captain's wartime experiences had made him conversant with rough and ready aid to the wounded, but the two made an odd spectacle as they drew their horses up at the Pillars half an hour later. Captain Trumbull was shirtless, as that fine piece of cambric had been torn into strips, one of which was bound picturesquely about the Major's head. Perkins was there, assisting Wyndham to dismount before Stacey could knock.

"I saw you coming, sir. What happened?"

Stacey's boots left chunks of mud on the parquet floor as he directed Wyndham's limping progress toward the stairs. "Get hot water ready and some bandages, Perkins. The Major's had a run-in with some unsympathetic rocks."

Wyndham protested weakly against all the fuss, but finally submitted to having his cuts cleaned and bandaged while Robert applied a healing salve.

"I'm not an invalid, Stace. Can't you trust me to wash myself?"

"Nurse Bunch will have my head if I leave you alone in here. It took a lot of talking to convince her that you didn't require her ministrations as well."

"God forbid. Just leave Robert with me and get yourself mended. Those hands look mauled."

"Don't worry about my hands. You should see your face."

"A few new scars to go with the old," Wyndham winced. "Don't look so concerned; I'm not dead yet. It will take more than an accident to finish me off."

"That's the thing," Stacey said thoughtfully. "I'm not so sure it was an accident."

"What are you talking about?"

"Someone was at the top of the cliff just before the rock fall."

"Who?"

"I don't know. I only saw his silhouette. But, Wyn, it's becoming obvious. Someone wants you out of the way—for good. And we needn't look far, if you ask me. It's the smugglers, of course."

The door closed softly behind him, leaving the Major to ponder that last remark. The thought wasn't a pleasant one, but it was no more than he suspected himself, although, unlike Stacey, Wyndham had a more specific villain in mind.

While the Major was easing his bruised muscles into the large four-poster bed, Samantha was just returning from a visit to the Newberrys, the tenants of Westbridge farm. It was a small act of defiance, but what possible objection could the Major have to her giving them a few dozen fresh eggs? Mrs. Newberry had recently delivered twins, and the extra food was much appreciated. Riding out on Pegasus was also a welcome relief after two days spent sitting

182

in her room, though with the dinner hour approaching, she'd best get back before the Major spotted her. She didn't care to meet him, as he had made no attempt at an apology, which she would not have accepted in any case. But his lack of repentance was provoking.

The short November dusk lay over the countryside when Samantha rode into the stableyard and was informed by an excited MacNamara of the Major's accident.

She tossed the reins down to him and dismounted. "What kind of accident?"

From Lady's stall Jem piped up angrily, "Covered with blood Lady was, and trembling like a leaf."

Samantha's eyes flew to MacNamara, who nodded in agreement. "'Twas a rockslide, Miss Sam. Like in the old days."

Waiting to hear no more, Samantha hurried into the house, a nightmare vision of the Major's torn and battered body haunting her. She met Stacey crossing the main hall and begged to know how serious were the Major's injuries.

"He's bruised and cut a bit, but there's no lasting damage done. He's a tough old war horse, you know."

"But how did it happen? MacNamara said a rockslide, yet you are unharmed."

Stacey had been thinking hard about this very subject, and he blurted out his feelings. "It wasn't an accident, Miss Crawford. Someone started that rockslide."

"What? How can you be sure?" she queried sharply.

"I saw a shadow up there only minutes before. Someone wants the Major out of the way. There was an incident in Brighton, too. He was set upon one night but managed to beat the ruffian off."

"That's just unbelievable. Who would want to harm him?"

"I'm sure it's the free traders, trying to scare him into silence. They want him to turn a blind eye to their use of the old manor. There's a lot of money at stake, and they know he's been asking questions, even talked to the preventive officer."

"But that's insane. Some of them are Crawford tenants. They wouldn't want to kill the Major."

By now Stacey had had time to regret revealing his suspicions to Miss Crawford. "I see I've upset you. I'm sorry. It's just that I am concerned for Wyn's safety, and I'm angry, too. After everything he is doing for these people . . ."

Busy with her own train of thought, Samantha did not ask what the Captain meant by his last words. "It must have been an accident. Rocks do fall by themselves sometimes. And as for the attack in Brighton, could it not have been a footpad?"

The Captain agreed gravely that it was possible, and Samantha went slowly up the stairs to her room, a worried frown creasing her forehead.

Wyndham came down for dinner despite Bunch's protests, alarming them all by the extent of his injuries. The bandage on his head was startlingly white against the ruddy brown of his hair, and the painful-looking bruise on his cheek was an ugly reminder of his close brush with death.

Wyndham frowned away all their solicitude, insisting he felt fine, but Hester declared that was clearly impossible. "And what about that nasty limp? I suppose your leg feels fine, too?" she snapped, masking her worry behind a show of irritation.

Samantha, deeply distressed by Captain Trumbull's revelations, had broken her self-enforced exile and come down to dinner also. Only her shadowed eyes indicated that she felt more than polite concern.

To Wyndham she appeared no more quiet than usual and just as aloof. She made no pretense of sympathy for his condition, and indeed, was behaving so coolly about it that he wondered just how much regret she might feel if the next "accident" were successful in eliminating him altogether.

Wyndham knew that was unfair of him; Samantha was not capable of malevolence. She might despise him as an ill-mannered savage, but she would never wish him harm. It was only that the Major had taken all he could of her silent condemnation. The reticence on his part was due to genuine perplexity. He wasn't sure if an apology would bring on another quarrel, or if she would even deign to acknowledge it. Besides, how could he apologize to someone who refused to come near him?

But Wyndham was plagued by the thought of another possibility. Jasper's threat to try something else might not be as simple as having Samantha lie for him. Had Dakins meant something far more sinister?

And since her cousin confided in her, could Samantha shed some light on this tangle?

Tired of the silent stalemate, the Major sent a message up to Miss Crawford shortly after dinner, requesting that she meet him in the library.

The message threw Samantha into a state of agitation. Was he going to apologize at last for his boorish and unforgivable behavior? Well, he would grovel before she forgave him, if she did at all. Donning one of her new dresses from Brighton and carefully brushing her hair into a smooth knot at her neck, she presented herself at the library door at ten minutes past eight and knocked only once before walking in.

The wound in his leg was throbbing as Wyndham faced Samantha across his desk, and the annoying pain made his brow draw together in a forbidding frown. "First, let me apologize for my behavior at the ball. It was inexcusable. I had no right to use you so badly."

Samantha nodded her head curtly, waiting for him to prostrate himself further. She was not about to make it easy for him.

The Major rubbed his knee. "I presume you know about what happened today. It wasn't an accident."

Taken aback by the abrupt change in topic, she answered in surprise, "Of course it was an accident. How can you think otherwise?"

"Because I am not a credulous fool," he snapped.

"Nonsense. You are seeing danger where none exists. No one could want to harm you."

"I wish that were true. I want you to tell me

exactly what Dakins said to you the night of the ball."

"I thought you heard it all," she said bitterly.

"Not quite. I need to know what Dakins is plotting."

"What are you saying, Major? That Jasper is trying to murder you? How absurd."

"It's no secret that the smugglers are nervous about my inquiries. I haven't made any secret of the fact that I intend to see an end to this crime on Crawford land. There is no doubt in my mind that it is the free traders who have arranged these attacks on me. Well, Miss Crawford? Will you help me to discover my enemies?"

Samantha was astounded. "You think I know anything about this . . . this imaginary plot?"

"You are their benefactor, Miss Crawford. You visit them with eggs from my hen house. You listen with sympathy to every tale of woe, whether it is the Huddleses or Jasper Dakinses. If you have heard anything, I would appreciate that information."

"How could you think such a monstrous thing of me?"

"You misunderstand, Miss Crawford. I thought perhaps one of the men might have let a word slip . . . a hint."

"That I kept safely hidden."

"Not knowingly."

"You are letting your suspicions run away with you, Major. I've known these people my whole life, and none of them would consider harming you. But if it is true, which I seriously doubt, my sympathy, even my concern for them, would not extend to closing my eyes to a crime."

"I think you truly believe what you are saying, Miss Crawford, and your defense of these people does you credit. But loyalty should not blind you to truth—even loyalty to your cousin Jasper."

"I . . . I don't know what you mean," she faltered.

"I mean, aren't your feelings for him such that you would ignore anything suspicious in his conduct?"

The unrelenting gaze leveled at her was not only an accusation but an indictment, and since he was so certain of Jasper's guilt, hers was a foregone conclusion, it seemed. The Major should have waited with his apology. She was going to give him reason to make a bigger fool of himself.

The Major recognized the martial light in Samantha's eyes. Since he had unleashed the Crawford temper in her, it seemed ready to ignite at the slightest provocation, though he preferred it to the cold aloof manner she had always assumed. At least a man could fight back at a virago; a marble statue was no kind of adversary at all.

"So you want the truth, Major Crawford. No proof, no denials, just the unvarnished truth. Very well. Jasper and I are plotting against you. I want the Pillars and only you stand in my way. Furthermore I am the ringleader of the smugglers. When you think I am safely in bed, I am secretly running a lugger through the channel and unloading French contraband. Yes, I am involved up to my indiscreet ears, Major. Is that the answer you want?"

He stood up from his chair and ignoring the pain

in his leg, stormed around the desk to grab her by the shoulders. "You damned idiot! Can't you see I'm trying to help?"

For a moment Samantha was held grip in a savage pleasure at his anger. She felt a breathless tremor of anticipation, waiting for the same explosive attack the Major had inflicted on her the night of the ball. But when the dark face, only inches from her own, showed no signs of repeating the disgusting performance, Samantha broke out of his hold.

"I don't want your . . . help," she said in a cold, tight voice. "I never did, if you will remember. And I will never forgive you for the false accusations you have leveled against me. It was a mistake to think you had any kind of human decency in you. But to my great relief, I do not have to tolerate your abuse any longer. I'm leaving as soon as arrangements can be made. And," she threw in for added measure, "if I cannot find a respectable position, I'm sure the free traders will have me."

Her head high, Samantha made a magnificent exit, leaving Major Wyndham Crawford to suffer the rankling frustration of having bungled things as badly as raw recruit.

CHAPTER 15

Jasper shivered in the doorway. The night was dark, and the slivered moon was mostly hidden by the clouds that promised rain before the dawn. Overgrown trees that encroached on one side of the old manor threw deep shadows that Jasper's anxiously watching eyes could not penetrate. Where were they? Long minutes passed and then cautiously moving figures detached themselves from the dark of the wood. They were coming. Opening the door wider, Jasper led the way down dusty steps to the cellars, the lantern swinging in his hand. In a few moments the stone-lined room under the house was filled with low-voiced men whose features were hard to ascertain in the feeble light of a single lantern.

"Where's Jed?"

"Comin', young sir, comin'."

The man swaggering down the stairs purposefully slowed his descent as if to emphasize that nothing could be started without him. And nothing could, Jasper thought resentfully, not when he had the rest of the men so terrorized.

Jed Pargins was a relative newcomer to the area

but in a short time had somehow clawed his way to the top. That state of affairs was already very much accepted by the time Jasper decided to seek his fortune at free trading, and he had only heard of the deadly fight for power between Pargins and the former leader, a local man. Since then, the men maintained a healthy respect for the sharp-edged blade that Pargins kept hidden beneath the voluminous folds of his greatcoat, for he was able to make it appear with lightning speed each time he felt the need to stress a point.

Jasper had told the tough, unpleasant ringleader that Major Crawford knew of the smugglers' use of the manor, so this was to be the last meeting of the gang in their secret hideaway.

Pargins had now taken his place in front of the group and lifted the lantern from Jasper's unprotesting fingers. "Boys, Mr. Dakins here turned us onto a good thing: this room, the cove, and the tunnel. Now I'm tellin' ye we're goin' to have to give it up."

There was a babble of protest at that and some shouted questions. "Why? What d'ye mean, Jed?"

"It's the Squire, lads. He don't like it, see? He don't care that yer hungry. He's hand in glove with that snoop, Travers."

"It ain't no skin off his nose! The old man never minded 'long as we sent along some brandy anyways," said one shabby fellow in black.

"Well, maybe I done somethin' to fix things," Pargins grinned, showing a mouthful of yellowed stumps. "Tomorrow night we're tryin' a new spot where the Major ain't goin' to bother us no more!"

That triggered much comment and a cry of, "How'd you do it?"

Smiling slyly, Pargins put a finger on the side of his nose. "Ask me no questions; I'll tell ye no lies! We'll signal the lugger from the beach by the quarry. Have the wagons lying ready, and we'll transport all straight on from there."

Mopes, a Crawford tenant, protested at that. "But, Jed, that ain't no good! Why, the Major's always hanging around that old quarry. Are ye crazy? He'll see we been there."

Pargins shook his head. "Yer a little bit behind times, lad. The Major won't go near that quarry! Once burned, twice shy. Ain't that so?"

Silence and shuffling feet greeted that assertion as the men took in Pargins's words.

"I'll even wager he don't turn us in if he does find out. Never fear, lads! I've warned off Mr. High and Mighty."

There wasn't a man in the room who didn't know about Major Crawford's narrow escape from the rockslide, but they had believed it to be only an accident. Pargins's disclosure left them stunned. Almost to a man they were Crawford tenants, and each of them felt a loyalty to the family that was nearly feudal. For generations Crawfords had seen to it that no matter how bad conditions were, no one actually starved. Every man had a roof over his head, and every child was sent to the village school until he was of an age to go to work. Admittedly in recent years things were bad enough, but despite old man Phineas's penurious ways, his granddaughter never forgot them. Even if it were only an offer of a loaf of bread, she continued her visits to each home. The new heir was a dark horse as yet, although he had moved the Huddles to a more respectable dwelling and, under cover of Miss Samantha, had freely given some money where it was most needed.

The mood in the damp cellar changed subtly. Pargins had gone too far. Maybe the new owner at the Pillars was a stranger, but he was a Crawford, after all. Rents went unpaid, but they were still on their farms, weren't they? If it came to that, Pargins was a stranger, too.

Jasper spoke for all of them. "You nearly killed him! I want no part of murder, Pargins. That's not what we're here for!"

Pargins glanced about, but there were no smiles for him now in the crowd. "Murder? Who said anything about murder? I just scared him off. If we're going to use the quarry tonight, I had to make it safe, didn't I?" There was a whining note of cajolery in his voice, but it worked. The men relaxed their air of guarded wariness. Placing a friendly arm on Jasper's shoulders, Pargins grinned ferociously, daring anyone to question his words.

Jasper said nothing more, but shrugged off the greasy sleeve that rested so uncomfortably around his neck. He didn't believe the man. If Major Crawford survived, it was merely a piece of luck. Sick at his stomach with the knowledge that it was his warning to Pargins that had prompted the attack, Jasper was intensely glad that this was his last operation with the free traders. He was quitting—if Pargins would allow it, he thought uneasily.

The promised rain had held off, and an early morning fog lay flat over the countryside, its gray, curling fingers hugging the ground. It was market day in the village of Little Ditchling, and those who had arrived early were setting up their stalls for the throngs that soon would be converging on them. This was the high point of the week for the local farmers as Little Ditchling offered the only crowd of size within six miles. Here could be found the freshest produce, the plumpest chickens, and the most complete assortment of cheeses, all saved by the farmers for this one day of the week.

Rumor had it that the peddlers who made the rounds of the small villages on market day carried a few items that miraculously had made their way across the Channel without a customs stamp. But since a French-made barrel was pretty much like an English one, and a good price for an authentic length of Lyons lace was hard to resist, they continued to sell their wares with few questions asked.

Doolittle had ridden down to the village this morning to look over some heifers that Squire Mainwaring had instructed his bailiff to sell. The Major agreed that the Crawford cattle needed an infusion of this improved strain, and he urged Doolittle to buy as many as he thought necessary.

The crowd was sparse at this hour of the morning, and Doolittle quickly made his way to the village center where the animals were penned for display.

He spotted Mainwaring's bailiff almost at once and was about to approach him when he noticed Jasper Dakins.

It was odd enough to find the boy here at this hour, but of even more interest to Doolittle was the young gentleman's companion. What was Dakins doing with a scalliwag like Jimmy Bristol? Their conversation seemed to be more in the nature of an argument, but in a short time Doolittle saw money change hands. Jasper nodded curtly, then hurried away, but Jimmy stopped to stow away his fistful of coins, giving Doolittle ample opportunity to cross over to him.

"And what are you up to this morning, you young scamp?"

The suddenness of Thomas Doolittle's question on top of his unexpected wealth jolted Jimmy into telling the truth for once. "I just rented out my mother's wagon."

"Then why is it sittin' by her stall, plain as day? I warn you, boy, if you do that lady out of her day's take, I'll thrash you myself."

The usual wheedle was back in his voice as Jimmy appraised his one-time employer with sly cunning. "My mother won't suffer for today's work. I got more in my hand now than a month of market days. Besides, he don't need the wagon till later."

"What does Dakins need with your wagon at all?"

Jimmy grinned. "I wouldn't want to be guessin' myself now, but I'll tell ye, it's not the first time his nibs has picked up the wagon at dusk and brought it back in the morning."

Supposedly no one was aware when an empty wagon was missing overnight from the barn, but it seemed Jimmy wanted payment for his silence. How much had he made from the "gentlemen" already, and where was Jasper Dakins getting the money to pay him?

"You're dealing with a bunch of dangerous cutthroats," the bailiff said dourly. "Be sure you don't push them too far."

But Jimmy only smiled at that warning, smug in the knowledge that Doolittle would do nothing about it. His confidence was such that he even issued a warning of his own. "If I was you, I'd be more worried about Dakins. I can take care of myself, but he's a green one yet." With that, he turned his back and sauntered away, insolence in every movement of his lithe young body.

Doolittle bought five heifers from Mainwaring's bailiff and arranged for their transport on the morrow. Bypassing the colorful stalls and, for once, refusing to stop and pass the time of day with any of the friendly faces calling out to him, he climbed into the trap and headed back to the Pillars.

The rain that had been threatening earlier developed into a fine mist that darkened the day into a premature gloom. Doolittle urged the pony to a trot, but by the time he reached home, both were covered with a glistening damp. Leaving the horse to MacNamara's ministrations, Doolittle strode to the scullery.

Samantha was filling her last days at the Pillars with the ordinary tasks that had occupied her over the years, as though the familiar routine could lessen the anguish of leaving her home forever. Now there was no question that her departure was anything but imminent. The Major had accepted her final burst of temper as the finish between them. Not that Samantha expected him to renew his offer for her to stay, but the security of knowing that she always had a home was now stripped from her. He wanted her gone, so she would go. Her Crawford temper might have brought her to a sorry pass, but her pride would not be trampled.

This morning as on most mornings now, she could be found in the kitchen, settling on the day's menu with Cook and deciding what would be needed from the village. As it was market day, the list was longer than usual.

Doolittle stood uncertainly in the doorway for a moment. "Miss Sam, can I speak to you?"

Handing the quill to Bunch to continue the list, Samantha accompanied the bailiff out into the yard and followed him across to his small quarters next to the stable. She had only an inadequate shawl to protect her from the chilly mist, though when she stepped inside, the meager fire that Doolittle had lit at six that morning hardly offered much warmth.

It was highly unusual for Doolittle to request Miss Samantha's presence in his office since the Major had taken over running the estate, and Samantha rightly assumed he had something of a serious nature to impart to her. His expression was solemn.

"I went to Little Ditching this morning. The Major wanted some of the Mainwaring cattle," he explained. "While I was there, I saw your cousin Jasper Dakins. It was early for him to venture out, so I was curious-like. You remember Jimmy Bristol? He's the lad I had to dismiss for theft . . . and it near broke his mother's heart, too." Doolittle paused and shook his head. "Well, Mr. Dakins and Jimmy had some business together this morning."

Samantha still had no idea where Doolittle was leading. "What does Jasper have to do with Jimmy Bristol?"

"That's what I wondered myself, miss. I asked the young scamp—Jimmy, that is—and he told me your cousin was used to rent his wagon from him . . . only at night." Doolittle's faded blue eyes pleaded with Samantha for understanding. "It's been goin' on for some time now, Miss Sam. They didn't know I saw them exchange some money, but I jolted Jimmy into confessing their dealings. Dakins is using the wagon tonight."

Samantha sighed deeply. "I'm not surprised, but Jasper promised me he'd quit after one more run."

"If that were all, Miss Sam, I wouldn't have bothered you. But while I was coming up the shore road, Jack Dotty passed me on his way to the village. He used to be the Colonel's man and liked army ways so well that he's taken up working with the preventives. I asked why he was up and about so early, and he said he was bringing a message for the riding officer at the temporary garrison in Little Ditchling. Dotty claims the smugglers are goin' to be stamped out once and for all, and that Lieutenant Travers is orderin' all the excisemen to be on the alert for to-night."

"Tonight!"

"I told him this was no weather for an honest man to be out in, but he declared it was the best kind for catching free traders. No man worth his salt couldn't take advantage of the rain to cover the sounds of an ambush." His grizzled head sagged despondently. "Many a good man will suffer the fate of a villain tonight."

Samantha understood that only too well. Of course, they must be warned. But how? Promising Doolittle she would think of something, she went back into the house and penned a note to Jasper. Forewarned, he might be able to stop the landing tonight, although Samantha doubted it. At best he might be able to change the appointed time, or the location. She did not want to consider the worst.

She sealed the note and rang for Robert. He could be trusted to hold his tongue, and Samantha impressed upon him the need for secrecy. The servants knew better than anyone what was planned for to-night, and hearing the urgency in Samantha's voice, Robert knew something was amiss.

"Where is the Major?" she asked cautiously.

"In Worthing, miss. He went to see the magis-trate."

Neither one of them doubted what that meant, and as Robert hurried out of the room, Samantha sank down at the escritoire with a groan of despair.

So the Major was in league with the preventives, after all. Samantha should have felt satisfaction that her low opinion of him was justified, but instead she was heartsick. How could he turn his back on the tenants without the slightest twinge of conscience, or was he troubled by his dual loyalties, one to his people and one to the law? Samantha felt no guilt at warning Jasper of the danger tonight, but she was haunted by a ringing accusation of complicity, which she denied, even struck out against. Never did she think it would be put to the test. But the Major had forced her hand. She had to do what she believed right. Besides, she owed him nothing. He had challenged her integrity, criticized her motives, and heaped on her the greatest insult a woman could bear. Then why, she thought piteously, could she not bring herself to hate him?

Somehow the slow hours of the morning passed, and Samantha joined her aunt at one, managing a fair semblance of her usual manner as she toyed with a light luncheon. Lady Fitz found her niece somewhat distracted, but aside from scolding her for not eating, let her be. The old lady was too deep in the megrims herself over the sad state of affairs between her two favorite people to do much more than pick at the excellent soufflé.

Worry kept Samantha on edge. Where was Robert? Surely he had found Jasper by now and should be returning with a message that all was taken care of. But when the ormolu clock on the mantel in the drawing room struck two, the footman was not yet back.

Samantha was about to give up hope when Stacey arrived. He had spent the morning with Elizabeth and only now returned to change for dinner at Dakins Hall. Samantha immediately inquired if he had seen Jasper today.

"Jasper? Why, no. Amelia was quite put out with him because he promised her some embroidery silks from the market and by the time I left her, was threatening dire punishments if he didn't return soon. Were you expecting him to call?"

Samantha said no, nothing like that, and Stacey went up to his room. She began to ponder the feasibility of riding in to Little Ditchling herself when a message was brought to her by one of the new maids that Robert was awaiting her in the back hall. Samantha hurried out to him, but when she saw the crumpled note in his hand, she knew her plan had failed.

"He weren't there, miss," the boy said breathlessly, "not nowhere. I went to the Hall first, but his man said he was gone from home. So then I rode into the village to search him out, but no one seen him. I did try, miss."

Samantha took the letter and thanked him. "You did your best, Robert. Now get into some dry clothes and have Cook give you a bowl of her hot soup."

Where to turn now? Jasper, along with the others, was headed for disaster. Samantha thought of a dozen wild ideas to save them, but none could be implemented without help. Someone with authority had to go to Lieutenant Travers. He'd never listen to a mere woman, especially with the Major working with him.

Captain Trumbull!

Samantha nearly ran up the stairs but slowed down at the door of his room. It would do no good to rush in and demand that he help her. He must be persuaded. Taking a deep breath, she knocked on his door.

CHAPTER 16

"It's mad! I can't do a thing like that! Why, if I weren't hanged, they'd lock me up in Bedlam."

"Not at all. Besides, if they found out, you could claim you were fooled as much as they."

"Top one lie with another. I see."

Samantha looked up at the troubled Captain, trying to gauge just how resistant he was to her scheme. Hiding her exasperation behind a winsome smile, she explained again. "Lieutenant Travers won't take my word, but he couldn't possibly doubt either your veracity or judgment."

"Only my sanity. Look, Miss Crawford, I know you think you are helping, but after all, Wyn knows just what he is about. Why don't you trust him to do what is best?"

Samantha dared not discuss the Major's views with his best friend. "All I want is to give them a chance to escape. You know what it will mean if they are caught."

Captain Trumbull ran his hands through his hair for the hundredth time. Miss Crawford was beyond reason. She wanted him to commit treason, or close to it, to save a gang of petty cutthroats. He understood neither her concern nor her methods. Leading the excisemen in the wrong direction was sheer insanity. How long did she think it would take Travers to realize he had been fooled?

"What makes you think the free traders are using the manor house, Miss Crawford?"

"I told you, the Major and I found proof of it, and he told the Lieutenant."

"So don't you think Wyn will have something to say about this when he finds out?"

Samantha's face lit up. "Then you'll do it?"

"Of course not."

"Then I'll go myself." Worn out with arguing, Samantha rose from the chair, but the Captain put a detaining hand on her shoulder.

"Don't be foolish, Miss Crawford. You can't take a risk like that."

Samantha regarded him in dismay. Not only would he not help her, but he was clearly determined to stop her from doing anything herself. It had been a bad mistake to confide in Captain Trumbull, for he believed that nonsense about a plot to kill the master of the Pillars. Yet . . . that might work to her advantage.

"What is risk when the Major's life might be at stake?" she asked.

"What do you mean?"

"Those attacks on him, Captain; you know he believes the free traders are responsible. Suppose he's right. Can you imagine their fury when they discover that the very night they were apprehended happened to follow the Major's visit to the magistrate in Worthing? His involvement with Lieutenant Travers is already known. And if he should be foolish enough to ride with the preventives tonight, do you think the blue coats of the riding officers will deflect a bullet meant for him? It would be a perfect opportunity for the smugglers to rid themselves of the man they will blame for their capture."

"For whom are you more concerned, Miss Crawford, the smugglers or Major Crawford?"

Samantha had no real answer to that. Of course, she placed no credence on the so-called attempts on the Major's life, but that didn't alleviate her worry for him. He would be placing himself in an awkward position if he rode against the free traders tonight. And that appeared to be exactly what he had in mind: another battlefield, with him leading the charge.

But his safety shouldn't be her concern. The Major forfeited that prerogative when he insulted her integrity. She owed him no consideration. It was Jasper and the others who merited her compassion.

"Does it matter?" she asked wearily.

The stricken look in her eyes was Stacey's undoing. "So you want me to lead the excisemen to the quarry."

The smile she gave him was enough to make him forget his qualms. "Yes. Tell them that you spoke to an informant today and discovered that the free traders have abandoned the manor house."

"And what if Wyn is with them?"

"Convince him as well. His life might depend on your persuasive abilities."

The only flaw Stacey could see in the plan was that once the Lieutenant realized he was being led on a wild goose chase, there was nothing to stop him from turning around and heading for the manor. The smugglers still could be caught there despite the delaying tactic.

Samantha had come to the same conclusion long before, but those few extra moments, an hour at the most, would give her time to get to the manor and warn the men herself.

She was not late yet, but Samantha knew there was little time to lose as she urged her hack carefully down the slippery and muddy lane that led to the old manor. The fine mist that sent trickles of cold down her back made it difficult to see. She had to trust the horse's instincts and her own memory of the way.

It was a night that most people would prefer to spend snugly at home, and Samantha was thankful that she had thought to borrow a pair of warm breeches from Robert so she could sit astride, secure in the saddle if old Pegasus should stumble in the deep ruts.

It had been easy for Samantha to slip out the side door and run back to the stables without anyone but Jem being the wiser. And she had sworn him to secrecy. Major Crawford had not returned to the Pillars before it was time to set out, and luckily Aunt Hester had retired to her room with a headache.

Dispatching Bunch to nurse the poor sufferer had been a last minute, but inspired, improvisation.

So far, so good. But still a worry to Samantha was the possibility that the Major was riding with the excisemen tonight. Captain Trumbull would never maintain that concocted tale of a disgruntled smuggler playing informer in the face of his friend's skepticism, and all depended on Stacey's convincing the Lieutenant that the free traders were using the quarry.

Shivering under the thin protection of her cloak, Samantha pulled the hood closer around her face. The wind was beginning to buffet the bare branches of the trees, but the mist was clearing at last, and a pale, lopsided moon was trying hard to shine between the patches of ragged clouds that scudded across the night sky.

Samantha had slowed Pegasus to negotiate a particularly steep incline when she heard the unmistakable whinny of a horse nearby. Looking back, she could just discern a rider coming at a good clip up the lane behind her. Just what she didn't want—company. Perhaps it was a smuggler heading for the manor. In that case she had nothing to fear. But it could be a preventive officer on patrol.

Knowing that in the dark, and in Robert's clothes, she was unrecognizable, Samantha still dreaded an encounter with the unknown horseman. Trying to reason away a rising panic, she urged her horse into a canter. But, alas, Pegasus had no wings. The rather elderly gelding was quite unwilling to increase his pace, and Samantha was forced to use her quirt on him. It was to no avail. A glance behind showed that her pursuer had gained appreciably. Indeed, Samantha's mount was no match for the other, but if she could reach the bend in the lane, she knew of a twisting path behind the hedgerow that led to the sea. Hidden in its deep shadows, she could wait until the other rider was safely by.

There was no doubt now. The horseman was determined to overtake her. The gap between them had narrowed to a few feet, and Samantha swung Pegasus to the left. Immediately a long arm reached out and grasped the bridle while a sharp voice ordered her to stop. She turned terrified eyes on the rider but only could see that he was not in uniform. Wrenching the reins from her fingers, he brought both horses to a shuddering halt.

The hood of her cloak had fallen back, revealing a mass of golden hair that had come undone and streamed about her face, but Samantha was too breathless to move.

"Meeting your friends for a bit of sport, Miss Crawford, or do you always take night rides dressed as a boy?"

"Major!"

"Correct." He dismounted and then lifted her to the ground, inevitably noticing the molded curves of her slender form. "Rather indecorous, those clothes, don't you think?"

Samantha gathered the cloak around herself to conceal the offending breeches, and pulled at the hood until it covered her hair. "Why were you following me?"

"Jem was worried. It seems everyone knows that there is mischief afoot tonight. Is that what brings you out, Miss Crawford? You did tell me you were the leader of the nefarious smuggling band. What did they do, leave you behind?"

He was standing very close, but Samantha was not daunted. "I've gone out for a late ride. No crime in that," she said defiantly.

"You picked a pretty night for it. I shall be glad to escort you home. Heroines have a dangerous time of it, I hear. Really, Miss Crawford, I thought better of your common sense." Going on in a severe tone, he added, "You have let your sympathies run away with you. This is not an adventure. So please pack up your good intentions and let those who know what is best manage things."

"What is best! Is it best that Huddle, Mopes, and, yes, Jasper die or . . . or be transported?"

The Major frowned. "No, of course not. I know you will find it hard to accept, but all is arranged. Your beloved free traders are safe, and I even dare hope that smuggling will cease in the neighborhood."

Samantha was amazed. "Then you have seen Captain Trumbull."

"Stacey? No, I have not laid eyes on him this day. I fear he would not approve of what I have done."

"What you have done . . . ? Oh, dear."

"You seem rather disturbed, Miss Crawford. Don't you believe I may have saved the day for your friends?"

"I don't understand your involvement at all, Major. Captain Trumbull was to be the one who saved

209

them. He is leading Travers and his men in the wrong direction this very instant."

"How did you manage to convince poor Stacey to do that? Never mind, I think I know. Poor Travers, too. You are an amazing woman, Miss Crawford, just as I've always said. But tell me, where is this fictitious rendezvous to take place?"

"At the quarry. We . . . or I thought that the tale of the landslide made it seem plausible."

"The quarry!" A look of horror came over the Major's face. "My God . . . of all places. It's plausible, all right. Only the fools are, in truth, using it tonight."

"But the manor . . ."

"I've no time to explain it now. Just pray I'm in time. Go right home, Samantha, and do not say a word to anyone." Then leaping into the saddle, he headed down the lane at breakneck speed.

Openmouthed, Samantha stared after him. She didn't understand any of this. But if the Major were to be believed, and the smugglers were indeed meeting at the quarry, she had betrayed the men herself by sending Captain Trumbull to the excisemen.

Climbing onto Pegasus's back once more, Samantha charged down the lane after him. She couldn't go home, not when it was her own impulsive actions that had placed everyone in the gravest jeopardy. As for the Major . . . that didn't bear thinking of. One fact, at least, was clear: Major Wyndham Crawford and she were on the same side, at last. But confound the man! Why didn't he tell her?

CHAPTER 17

Wyndham pressed Lady on, but the darkness made real speed impossible. Turning in frustration from the hedge-shrouded lane, he guided his mare over a rough track to the beach where the faint moonlight would allow him to gallop. There were hazards there, too, though the packed sand was easier going.

Blast all interfering women! His plan was in ruin now because of Samantha, but the Major couldn't help a surge of admiration for her audacity. Who would have thought that the drab, quiet spinster he met when he first came to the Pillars was a firebrand underneath. She'd be a worthy comrade-in-arms, although the Major wished she had been a little less daring tonight. Didn't she consult anyone besides the softhearted Stacey before she charged into the fray? Not even her cousin? He could have told her a thing or two.

It was late last night when Major Crawford answered an insistent rapping on the library window and allowed Jasper a furtive entry. Crawford was suspicious at first, but after hearing what the boy had to say, he understood Jasper's need for secrecy.

It had taken Dakins some time to come to the point of his nocturnal visit, but he finally explained that the Major had an "enemy."

"It's not you, I take it," Wyndham said with some reservation.

"Oh, no, sir." Jasper appeared genuinely startled by the notion.

"Perhaps you'd best tell me who it is then."

And haltingly Jasper did. He finished up earnestly. "Call me a rogue, if you will. I wouldn't blame you. But I'll not be a party to murder. I'm getting out as I promised Samantha."

"Ah, yes. Your conspiracy with Miss Crawford. May I ask exactly what you had in mind when you convinced her to lie to me?"

"Lie?" Jasper thought seriously for a moment. "Not lie precisely. I only wanted her to keep the next run a secret . . . at least, my part in it. She told me that you covered my tracks over that business of the lantern, and for that I'm truly grateful. But I didn't think your benevolence would extend to letting me have one more go at it. Sammie was against the idea, but I rather forced it on her. She's so honest, I knew you would believe anything she told you." Jasper didn't notice the strained expression that appeared on the Major's face. "Anyway, it's lucky for you that I stuck with it, or I never would have discovered what Pargins had in mind. He's the one who started that rockslide."

Jasper's explanation had the ring of truth, certainly more so than the disturbing conclusion Major Crawford had come to. Of course, Samantha would not recognize a threat of murder in her cousin's words; none was there.

"It is understandable that the ringleader of such a group would want to see me out of the way, especially as you tell me he is a hardened criminal. But what about the others? Are they not a party to this scheme also?"

"Never! I don't blame you for looking skeptical, Major. I admit there has been little about my conduct in this to earn your trust. But the rest of the men are good people. I've known them my whole life. They were appalled when Pargins admitted his culpability at the quarry. Of course, he told them it was just to frighten you off, but as I said, I overheard him with one of the men . . . not a tenant. Next time he intends to complete the job."

"If there is a next time. What would you say if I told you that Lieutenant Travers already knows about tomorrow night?"

"How?"

"One of the smugglers, not a local man obviously, traded the information for a fat purse and a pardon."

"I see your point, Major. I could just be playing for a last-minute reprieve myself by betraying my comrades."

The Major regarded Dakins's bitter smile and saw no guile there. His original assessment of Jasper as a somewhat weak and spoiled young man was nearer the mark than crediting him with the cunning evil of a master plotter. It was Samantha's infatuation with her cousin that had aroused the Major's misgivings, and he admitted to himself now that much of it was based on his displeasure with Samantha herself.

"Not at all, Mr. Dakins," the Major said abruptly. "If you were involved in the plot, coming here to warn me would be putting yourself in great danger."

"That is generous of you, Major. But I only know that I could not have lived with my conscience otherwise."

"I believe you."

Those simple words removed the cloud from Jasper's face, if not the guilt from his heart. The Major wasn't the cold autocratic statue of propriety Jasper had assumed him to be, but a quite decent fellow up against a highly unorthodox situation. Major Crawford's next statement won him further approbation.

"Since you have put your life on the line, so to speak, by coming to me, I think it only fair to tell you that I am not uncaring of the plight of my tenants." The Major then went on to explain his scheme for reviving the economy.

"That is quite a plan," Jasper acknowledged. "And one that is sure to win you everlasting loyalty. But what of the immediate problem? Unless we can think of something quickly, the men won't be around to enjoy the benefits of your endeavor."

"You despair too easily, Mr. Dakins. Can't you send word to the French to postpone the rendezvous?"

"Impossible! Our contact would never reach them in time."

"And your friend Pargins can't be convinced to

cancel, I take it? All right. Then we must take a bit of evasive action ourselves. The preventives plan to station themselves at the old manor tomorrow night, but if—"

Jasper broke in excitedly. "Why didn't I think of it before? We're not using the manor house. Pargins wants to take advantage of the beach road and use the quarry as a landing stage for this run. That was why . . ." His words trailed off.

The Major nodded. "That makes it simple."

Now, as he sped through the night, Wyndham thought of his rash promise. Thanks to Samantha, if he did not arrive in time, Dakins and the rest of the men would be trapped between the troopers and the sea, and it would appear that Major Crawford had deliberately plotted to betray them. Lashing the tired mare, Wyndham galloped across the sand. High tide was but an hour away.

After rounding the last headland on the narrowing beach, the Major came to the sandy road that meandered from the quarry into Little Ditchling. There was no sign of trouble yet, but as he pulled up at a break in the cliff walls, a dozen or so men stepped out to surround him silently. He recognized a few faces, but most were grim-faced strangers. Jasper was not among them.

A squat figure in a ragged greatcoat spoke up. "And to what do we owe the honor of yer visit, Squire? We ain't partial to strangers jist droppin' in. Ye should've stood in bed tonight, me fine sir."

The crowd pressed closer, and Lady tossed her head in nervous dislike of the atmosphere.

Was this Pargins, Wyndham asked himself? It was too dark to discern his features, but the voice was vaguely familiar. Looking out over the hostile crowd, the Major sought a known face. "I'm here to warn you. There's been a mistake. Lieutenant Travers and his men will be here at any moment. Just leave the wagons and go home."

"Mistake! I'll venture it was yers," the man laughed raucously. "Do ye hear that, lads? The Squire is worried about ye. That's real nice, that is. But what makes my nose twitch is how he knowed we was here. Someone's been blabbing, I'm thinkin'."

There was a growl from the crowd at that, but the Major roared out in his parade-ground voice, "If you value your lives, you'll go home. Now!"

Some of the men took fright at his words and began to back off, but Pargins shouted at them. "Hold! I don't believe the Squire's warning. I say he's been sent to spy on us. Barnes, get me a rope. Dead men don't talk. Am I right, lads?"

An ominous silence followed, and a few men gathered around the Major, one burly fellow taking Lady's bridle in hand. Where were the loyal tenants that Samantha swore would not see him harmed? For that matter, where was Jasper? But the Major was not one to break at the threat of death.

"Don't be fools," he rapped out. "There's still a chance if you make haste. And as for you," he turned to Pargins, "you'd be wise not to make more trouble."

Pargins's eyes blazed with excitement, and his lips

216

stretched into an ugly smile. "Oh, I'll see there's no more trouble. Jump him, lads. He's unarmed."

"Stop!"

The shouted command from the back of the crowd stopped the men in their tracks. Jasper stepped forward, his face pale but resolute. He seemed to take heart from the way the men instantly obeyed his order, and when he turned to face them, his voice held a newfound confidence.

"Major Crawford is telling the truth. He's not here to betray you. Someone else has already done that."

A babble of excitement broke out, but Jasper still had the upper hand. "He has only your best interests at heart. Listen to him."

"Why should we believe Crawford?" called a voice. "He could easily be lyin' to us. He ain't done nothin' since he's been here."

"You're wrong," Jasper answered. "The Major is reopening the quarry. There'll be work for everyone, and better than the old days."

There was a murmur of surprise and a few nudges from some of the men who claimed to have suspected as much. It certainly explained why the Major had been showing such an interest in the place. If he were willing to sink his blunt into starting the quarry up again, there must be something to be made out of it . . . for everyone. Besides, the man was a Crawford, wasn't he? And as such had a lot more right to be ordering their lives than Pargins. Suspicious eyes traveled to their leader as the men pondered this new turn of events.

Pargins sputtered a curse, but Crawford gave him

no opportunity to speak again. "Huddle, get the wagons out of sight. And you, douse that lantern. There will be no signal for the French to spot tonight. Jasper, there isn't time for you to ride all the way back to Dakins Hall. Go to the Pillars and tell Miss Crawford that you will be spending the night. And if anyone should happen to ask," he smiled, "you've been in bed since ten."

With a cheeky grin, Jasper spun his horse around and disappeared into the night. The men began to move the wagons under the cover of the chalk cliffs, and within moments only Major Crawford and the deposed leader of the smugglers were left on the deserted road.

"You'll pay for this," Pargins growled.

The Major only spared him a passing glance, then giving Lady a light tap on the flanks, headed back up the long stretch of beach.

From her hiding place behind some fallen rock, only a few feet above, Samantha had heard everything. She was still shaking from the terror of it. How close the Major had come to losing his life because of her senseless stupidity. That horrible man might have succeeded in killing him if Jasper hadn't intervened. If only she had believed Major Crawford. Those attempts on his life were planned, not accidental, as she so callously determined. It must have been Pargins all the time. Yet it could have been Jasper just as easily, Samantha admitted to herself with painful candor. At least, by his actions tonight, Jasper had proven his innocence, but even that could not assuage Samantha's remorse. She had misjudged Major Crawford . . . on every count.

Wondering bitterly if she would ever be forgiven this night's work, she felt for a toehold, then inched up to peer cautiously at the solitary man on the beach. He was an evil-looking character as he stood there, his gaze fixed on the Major's retreating back. Samantha stifled a cry when he drew a long-nosed pistol from his coat, but she was already scrambling up the slope as Pargins mounted his horse and began following Lady's clearly defined hoofprints in the wet sand.

Pegasus was tethered to a tree stump at the bend of a footpath that wound around one side of the quarry. Racing back up to him, Samantha grabbed the reins and whipped him into a gallop. The curve of the beach below gave her about a quarter of a mile advantage over Pargins, but only if she could guide the old horse across the rocky terrain then ride him down the side of a cliff.

The Major was about to turn off the beach and head up the winding lane to the Pillars, when he heard someone calling his name. He looked back to see Samantha galloping madly down the steep slope. The hood of her cloak was whipped from her head, and a stream of fair hair gleamed silver in the moonlight. The Major did not seem to appreciate the picture she made.

"What are you doing here? I told you to go home."

For once Samantha did not take umbrage at his peremptory tone. "That man," she gasped. "He has a gun."

Crawford turned to look back along the beach just as a shot whistled by his head. He ducked low and shouted for Samantha to get moving. "I'll follow."

She dug her heels into Pegasus's heaving sides and set off, breathing a little prayer that the old horse would be able to keep up this unaccustomed pace. The Major, after one more glance behind, lined himself between Samantha and the muzzle of Pargins's gun.

Two more shots rang out in quick succession, and with the second Wyndham felt a sharp stab of pain. The jolt of it knocked him off-balance for a moment, but he swiftly righted himself, feeling for the extent of the wound. His fingers came away from his shoulder smeared with blood. The bullet had gone deep, but worse than the ragged hole was the loss of blood. Soon he would be too weak to control the horse, much less speed her toward home. And once Lady sensed his flagging energy, she would take her own direction. Wyndham was willing to risk a chase with Pargins if Samantha could get away. But even with her expert handling, it was becoming obvious that the old nag would never make it to the Pillars.

"The tunnel!" he called out to her, seeing Pargins veer toward the upper road that led to the Pillars.

Immediately Samantha swung to the right. It was high tide now, and the plunging breakers raced along the beach to lap around Pegasus's stumbling hooves. The horse shied, but Samantha held him firm across the rocky beach that led to the cove. Here was even less space to maneuver the horse between cliff sides and sea, but the tunnel was just ahead. Only a few more steps.

The Major would have wasted precious minutes searching for the entrance that was hidden in the rocks, but following Samantha's lead, he rode up to the second outcropping of boulders and dismounted.

She pointed to the opening. "Here. Hurry."

By now Wyndham was feeling dizzy. He walked across the sand steadily enough, but once inside the tunnel he stumbled against the wall. Samantha heard and reached out to take his hand in the darkness, when her fingers encountered the sticky wetness of blood.

CHAPTER 18

"You've been shot," she exclaimed in horror.

"A scratch, no more. Get the lantern."

For a few panicky seconds Samantha's hands fumbled over the rough stone wall, searching for the shelf that held the lantern. Then she touched cold metal. In the total darkness of the tunnel it took some time before she was able to coordinate flint and wick, but at last the candle was lit. Holding the lantern high, she turned to examine her companion: He looked almost normal as he leaned tiredly against the opposite wall.

"Let's go back to the secret room," she suggested. "You'll be more comfortable there, and we can see to that arm of yours."

"I'd rather stand watch here. We lost Pargins earlier, but that's not to say he won't come looking for us. Besides Travers should be here soon . . . unless Stacey is more persuasive than I gave him credit."

Samantha was about to apologize for involving his friend, but the Major suddenly looked ready to collapse. His jacket was already stained with blood, and now his face was ashen. This was all too much on top of the wounds he had sustained at the quarry. He had removed the head bandage, but his leg must still be painful. "Never mind the others for now," she said. "I am more concerned for you." And she led him unprotesting up the narrow passageway.

Upon reaching the nail-studded door to the room, Samantha opened it and shone the light about. It was dank and barren of comfort, and her heart misgave her for an instant. Then putting on a brave face, she took charge.

"Sit down on that box, please, and give me your handkerchief," she ordered. "I'll bind up your wound."

"I tell you, it's nothing," the Major protested, but she was already easing off his bloodstained coat and examining the nasty gash in his upper arm.

Fortunately the bullet had gone through, although the jagged tear was seeping blood at an alarming rate. No wonder the Major was being so uncharacteristically meek. Samantha marveled that he was even conscious. Taking his linen handkerchief, she folded it into a pad and, with a strip torn from his ruined shirt sleeve, bound his arm tightly. Using another piece of cloth, this one from the tail of her own shirt, she then fashioned a rough sling. The slightest movement would start the wound bleeding again, she feared, but it was the best she could do for now.

The Major sat silent under Samantha's ministrations, marveling at her presence of mind. Most women would have fainted at the sight of so much blood. But Samantha wasn't most women. She was stubborn to the point of unreasonableness, but never unkind. And even though she was dressed as a boy, something no other female of his acquaintance would ever dream of doing, she had never seemed so alluring. Altogether a highly unusual woman.

Samantha noted his regard and flushed self-consciously. She must look hoydenish with her windblown hair and dressed in Robert's ill-fitting jacket and breeches. Lowering her eyes, she slipped the Major's coat over his good arm and buttoned it up across his chest.

"Is that better?"

"Yes, thank you." He tried to take Samantha's hand, but she turned away.

"I think it would help too if you sat on the floor here and leaned against this box," she replied in a brisk tone.

Then she insisted on spreading Robert's jacket on the dirt floor before allowing the Major to settle himself comfortably. But when she began to cover him with her own cloak, he protested that she would be too cold without it and demanded that she join him under its protection.

The Major never would have been so daring were he not feeling light-headed. Neither did he question Samantha's meek acceptance of his offer. The frightened girl nestled so cozily against his shoulder was not the infuriating Miss Crawford who plagued his days and haunted his nights. This was the sweet dream that had always eluded him.

Samantha, too, wondered at her own temerity. This was not her usual behavior with Major Crawford, and she feared he could feel the mad pounding of her heart. She tried to concentrate on the peril of their situation, but when the Major, in his feverish state, touched his lips to her hair, she gave in to the bittersweet joy of the moment.

"Warm now?" he murmured.

If he could have seen her flushed face, the Major would have been inspired to investigate the reason, but Samantha kept her face averted and mumbled in assent.

When she did manage a peek at him, she became frightened by the beads of moisture on his brow. He caught her scrutiny and smiled into her eyes. "If I thought you wouldn't hit a man when he's down, I'd risk kissing you again."

Samantha knew it was delirium that was making him speak so absurdly, but that did not prevent her heart from turning over at the expression on his face. Her understanding had come too late, though. Yet even if she had faced the truth of her heart, what good would it have done her? Wyndham Crawford did not return her feelings. He would probably never forgive her for tonight. Still the tender expression in his eyes played havoc with her senses, and she raised her lips to his with a thrill of anticipation. The Major sighed and dropped his head to her shoulder, where his eyes closed and he fell off in a doze. Dispiritedly, Samantha rested her head on top of his and prayed for Travers to come.

As the guttering candle threw moving shadows on the walls, Samantha almost succumbed to the wild fancies that lurked in the corners of the dark, underground room. Every passing moment seemed an endless hour to her taut nerves, and the worst was facing her terrible feelings of guilt.

It was her fault and hers alone that the Major had been shot. If only she had listened to Stacey's assurances that his friend knew what he was doing. Instead she had blundered in and, perhaps, cost the Major his life. At least he had warned the others in time. But that was no solace when he may have given up his own life in the process. And that might be the outcome unless Lieutenant Travers arrived soon. But what if he decided not to search the tunnel? Captain Trumbull might have convinced him only too well that the smugglers had abandoned the manor house. And if they went to the quarry and found it deserted, the excisemen might already be back in their safe, warm beds.

Finally a new fear, that the candle would burn out and leave them in the dark, made Samantha wake her companion. "Major," she breathed in his ear. "Wyndham."

"My golden Diana," he murmured, opening his eyes to the vision of a tender face framed by blond curls.

Samantha gazed at him in distress. He was really delirious now. "Major Crawford, we must leave. Obviously no one is coming, and it's dangerous to wait any longer."

"Why?" he asked and sat up, wincing slightly.

"The candle is almost out, and you must see a doctor."

The Major threw a weary glance at the stub that

remained in the lantern. "We haven't been here that long."

"Even so," she argued, "I would feel safer elsewhere. If we could just go up into the manor house . . . or better still, let me take your horse and go for help."

"You are determined, I see. Very well. Help me up. But both of us will leave together. I don't fancy your riding alone with Pargins still on the loose."

"But how will you manage with only one arm? No, it's best if I go alone."

"Are you defying me again, Samantha?"

She met his gaze squarely. "Only for your own good."

"Yes, that is always your argument—everything you do is for someone else's good."

"I take full blame for tonight's mishaps, Major. But you could have given me some indication that you were not as heartless as you appeared."

"I thought I was exceptionally nice from the very beginning."

But before Samantha could answer, a scuffling sound in the passageway brought her scrambling to her feet. "It must be Travers."

The Major put up a detaining hand. The furtive movements outside the door did not suggest a troop of soldiers. With a grunt of effort, he pulled himself upright and pushed Samantha none too gently into the corner where she would be shielded by the opening door. Then he sat down on the wooden crate and positioned the lantern so that it threw its feeble light forward, leaving him in shadow.

The door swung open, but for a moment it seemed no one was there. Then a cocked pistol and a tousled head were poked cautiously around the jamb. Seeing Major Crawford sitting casually on a box, a nasty grin split Pargins's face, and he stepped boldly into the room.

"Well, well. Ye made it easy for me. Not even a sword do ye have," he gloated.

Wyndham had been bitterly regretting the lack of a weapon all evening. Still he had one advantage: Pargins had tossed his own candle into the passageway, and the lantern on the floor was the only illumination. In the dark things might be more equal. Maneuvering for time, the Major spoke scornfully.

"I wouldn't be so sure of myself if I were you, Jedidiah Parr."

"Ye remembered, after all. I thought it had slipped your mind. But it don't make no difference. I jist got two scores to settle with you now, that's all."

The Major's gaze never left Parr's face. Not by a flicker of an eyelid did he acknowledge Samantha's presence behind the door. He shrugged disdainfully. "The only score you'll settle is at the end of a hangman's rope."

Parr took a threatening step closer. "Still as proud as Lucifer, I see. Well, I'll soon change that."

"You're a doomed man, Parr. Travers and his troops are on their way here, so even if you manage to kill me, they'll clap you in irons the minute you step foot outside."

"Yer threats don't mean nothin' to me, Major." Unwittingly he slipped back into the old form of address. "I got ye over the barrel of a gun, so all yer fancy talkin' ain't goin' to do ye no good."

"I believe you are a coward after all," the Major jeered. "Take away your weapon, and you're a sniveling crybaby . . . like the last time," he added softly. "Remember last time, Sergeant, when I found out about your selling military stores to civilians? You begged me not to have you shot. Why, you even went on your knees to me."

Parr's thick hand shook with fury. "Ye lie! I'd never crawl to the likes of ye. There was no chance of me bein' shot. It was the stockade all the time."

The Major only gave him a look of pity mixed with scorn. "Is that how you remember it, Parr? Odd that it's not on the record that way."

"I never begged ye," Parr shouted, goaded into a fine fury. "And I'll put an end to yer lyin' ways once and for all."

He was well into the room now, leaving the door invitingly clear, and Wyndham gave Samantha an almost imperceptible nod. But Samantha was rooted to the spot. Even if her life depended on it, which it very well might, she couldn't take those two steps to freedom and safety. To run away while the Major faced death at the hands of this beast was unthinkable. It was most quixotic of Wyndham, and Samantha's eyes filled with tears, but she had no desire to save herself at such a cost.

Major Crawford's arm was bleeding again, and his face looked deathly white. Samantha knew if she didn't do something quickly, there'd be no need to worry about Parr's threats. She had already discarded the idea of surprising the man from behind, to divert him enough so that the Major could overcome him. Wyndham barely had the strength to stand, much less fight. He'd be felled in seconds. But there was another possibility. If Parr thought she were armed . . .

Stepping swiftly out of her hiding place, Samantha kicked the door back forcefully against the wall. As she hoped, the noise brought the Major's assailant whirling around.

"Drop that pistol!" she demanded in her gruffest tones.

In the dim light of the dying candle, Parr could only see that he was caught between two men. Damn! He had forgotten that the Major had someone with him when he rode across the beach. The pistol wavered uncertainly in his hand.

Taking advantage of the distraction, the Major knocked over the lantern, and instantly, the room was plunged into utter darkness. Shouting, "Sam, get out!" he dived for Parr's knees, sending them both sprawling to the floor.

In the midst of the confusion a shot was fired, and in the stone-lined room the sound echoed deafeningly. Samantha pressed herself close to the wall, unhurt but terrified. She had lost all sense of direction in the overwhelming blackness, and felt as though she were struck both deaf and blind. Every instinct clamored for her to scream out Wyndham's name, to know if he were still alive, but before she could make a sound, the room was filled with a blinding light.

Blue-coated soldiers seemed to be everywhere, and one voice nearby asked, "Is he dead?"

Samantha let out a strangled moan.

"Good God! It's Miss Crawford! Are you all right, ma'am?" Captain Trumbull queried anxiously.

His voice sounded strangely far away, and she wondered detachedly if she were about to faint. "Wyndham?" she asked. "Is it the Major?" Then she saw him lying on the dirt floor. "No!" she cried and fell to her knees beside him.

Lieutenant Travers was saying something to her, but she couldn't attend to him. Her hand reached out to touch the still, white face of Major Crawford, and only then did she realize that he was breathing, alive, but unconscious.

"He's going to be all right, Miss Crawford, but he must be taken home at once," Travers was explaining patiently.

"Yes, I understand."

"I've sent a man to fetch a conveyance from the nearest farm. In the meantime could you please tell me what happened? Why are you here?" And dressed so outlandishly, he added to himself, too much the gentleman to voice such a comment.

Samantha stared at the Lieutenant dazedly, quite incapable of manufacturing a plausible explanation. Captain Trumbull came to her rescue.

"The young lady is in a state of shock, Lieutenant. I suggest you hold all questions until tomorrow. By then the Major may be able to shed some light on tonight's events." And for me, as well, Stacey thought. Even he was nonplussed to find Samantha here with Wyn, although by now the Captain knew there had been a change of plan.

The Lieutenant looked suspicious, but acquiesced. "Yes, I suppose so. Though it is all most unusual."

"It is all my fault," Samantha murmured to Stacey.

Coughing loudly, he took her arm and shook it. "Miss Crawford is beside herself with worry," he explained hastily. "Completely overcome."

A makeshift stretcher was fashioned by the soldiers from their muskets and blue coats, and they lifted the Major onto it carefully, while a cursing Parr, already in irons, waited between two sturdy guards.

Placing his own cloak around Samantha's shoulders, Captain Trumbull noted how her shadowed eyes followed Wyndham's removal. He endeavored to comfort her. "It is well that he is unconscious. The trip home won't be so painful."

"It will be for me, Captain," she whispered.

CHAPTER 19

It had taken two days of anxious nursing, but very soon Major Crawford was on the mend. The doctor came by to check on his progress and was so well pleased that the master of the Pillars was allowed to sit up for a while and receive visitors. Lieutenant Travers, who had been kicking his heels downstairs for a day and a half, was ushered up to the sickroom to see the patient.

"Well, Lieutenant, I have you to thank for my life, they tell me." The Major was propped up in bed, pale, but smiling as he held out his good hand.

"No need to thank me. We cut it rather fine, after all. But how are you, sir? You're looking surprisingly well. That jolting ride home had us pretty scared for you. Miss Crawford sat there holding you steady, as game as you please, else you might have bled to death."

"Did she? I hadn't realized. Tell me, what happened at your end of things? Did you catch the smugglers?"

"It was a damned disappointing evening, taken all in all. At least we have this Pargins-Parr fellow. He

233

was the leader of the smuggling ring on this section of the coast and no friend of yours by all accounts. We've got enough witnesses to hang him twice over. Who is he anyway?"

"He was a master sergeant under me three years ago in Spain. I had him court-martialed; that was his grievance against me. It seems he escaped from prison and made his way here."

"Right to your doorstep, so to speak. The old house was a perfect setup for him."

"Hmm. What I don't understand is why you and your troops weren't at the manor house when I arrived. I was rather depending on that, you know."

"Were you, sir?" The Lieutenant quirked an eyebrow. "Then I wonder why your friend, Captain Trumbull, thought we should proceed to the quarry."

"He was given false information, as I understand," the Major explained.

"Yes. I can safely presume that much," Travers said dryly. "It was set up to appear that way, though, for when we arrived at the quarry, we found some farm wagons pulled up into the shadow of the cliff, and a French lugger, by her cut, was hanging about offshore. We stationed ourselves out of sight and waited until high tide had come and gone, but no one showed. The Frenchie moved off eventually, and there was no landing that night. The smugglers obviously had been warned we were in the neighborhood, for when we decided to check the tunnel, on the chance that they had used it after all, there was no sign that anyone had been there except for you and Miss Crawford . . . and Pargins, of course."

"Did Miss Crawford explain that she set out to warn me about Pargins?" Wyndham said carefully.

"She did tell us how Pargins shot you, that you both then took shelter in the tunnel because her horse had gone lame, and how Pargins tracked you down and threatened you. Miss Crawford seems to be a remarkable woman, although I can't fathom why she blames herself for your predicament."

Lieutenant Travers was curious. There was some mystery here, but he didn't think it had anything to do with the smugglers. It was pretty clear that Miss Crawford was more than a little fond of the Major. But what had made her go running off in the night in her footman's clothes was a puzzle . . . and why to the quarry?

Wyndham weighed the problem of how much to reveal of the evening's events. He sat silent for a moment, then turned to the Lieutenant. "I can't tell you all that occurred. But you're a married man, Travers, and you know what queer starts the ladies have now and again. I rely on your discretion in this matter."

Flattered, the Lieutenant made haste to assure the Major of his tomblike silence on all not directly related to his duty.

"I have reason to believe that some, if not all of my tenants, were involved in Parr's smuggling gang. I say *were*, Travers, not *are*. As you know, the Pillars has been grossly neglected of late, and the old man turned a blind eye on all such goings-on. I feel quite

235

differently about it. With all the information that slipped across the Channel along with English gold during the war, I can't accept smuggling as an innocuous game. When I came to the Pillars some two months ago, my man of business warned me of the situation, and I vowed to put a stop to it. But there's no use fooling myself; French brandy is the only cash crop my farms have been harvesting this long while."

Travers sat silent, his bright, inquisitive eyes fixed on the Major.

"When I came to you two days ago, and you told me about the raid, Lieutenant, I thought of my tenants. Say what you will, I have a responsibility there. So I rode to the magistrate in Worthing that morning and asked him if I could stand bond for any of them who were caught in your dragnet."

"Very decent of you, sir. But how do you suppose the smugglers found out that we were going to strike last night? Not from you, I know, sir. But someone must have warned them."

"Perhaps the same character who sold the information to you originally."

"And he purposely told your friend to give me the wrong direction?"

"It seems a possibility," Wyndham remarked blandly. "At least, there is no doubt that Stacey was gulled."

"Miss Crawford, too?" Travers asked politely.

"Definitely, Miss Crawford, too. At any rate there will be no more French luggers off-loading on my property, Lieutenant, and neither the quarry nor the manor will be used by such again. I'm opening a manufactory on the site of the quarry. A cement works, and it should provide a living wage for any man in the neighborhood who is willing to work."

"That's good news, Major, good news indeed. But your nurse is frowning. I must not overtire you. Need I add that Miss Crawford's name shall not appear in my report?"

"Thanks, Travers. You're a good sort."

Wyndham sank back on his goose-down pillows, exhausted. The fever had weakened him, no mistake. Thinking over what had been said, he felt reasonably certain that he had handled Travers well. There would be no repercussions despite a few unanswered questions. Smuggling, as far as his people were concerned, was finished business. Luckily the Lieutenant was too much the gentleman to press for details that might prove embarrassing to Samantha.

Drowsily he smiled up at nanny Bunch who had tiptoed in to lay a hand as light as a withered leaf on his forehead. So Samantha had held him on the road home. Dear, good girl, he thought and fell asleep.

It was the next day before nanny Bunch allowed the Major another visitor. This time it was Captain Trumbull.

"How are you, you old faker? Sick call again today?"

"Blame Bunch, not me. I'm nearly fit."

The first topic of conversation between the two friends was their plans for opening the quarry and the establishment of a plant to process the limestone and clay into cement. Stacey had agreed to go shares in the venture and to manage the business, as well.

"We'll make our fortunes, see if we don't, Wyn! The market for cement is potentially immense."

"And there's not a man I'd rather have as partner, that's certain," the Major smiled.

"I've got some good news, old man. Probably you've seen it coming. I'm a damned lucky fellow, y'know," Stacey stammered self-consciously.

"No! You and Elizabeth? Famous! Well, we must see about finding a suitable house in the neighborhood. Miss Crawford will be very pleased."

Stacey beamed inarticulately and crushed the proffered hand until Wyndham yelped. "Give over, Samson. I might need that paw of mine again."

The Major was very happy for his friend, although his own affairs seemed to be progressing at a much slower pace. Everyone managed to wander in and out of his room with annoying regularity except the one person he was longing to see. Lady Fitz drove him nearly wild by checking on him almost every hour and plumping up his pillows with ruthless determination. Even Jem sneaked past nurse Bunch's ceaseless guard to reassure the Major that Lady was in fine fettle, although Pegasus was lame and had to be turned out to pasture.

Wyndham's patience was worn out by the end of the week when he finally asked Bunch if Miss Crawford had recovered from the rigors of last Thursday night's adventures.

"Happen she's fit enough," nanny Bunch sniffed. "But I don't hold with such goings-on. She went behind my back, sir, and it's a wonder you weren't both kill't. It was the Lord's mercy, and so I told her."

"She's a fine woman, Bunch. Brave as a lion."

Nanny looked at him sorrowfully. Gentlemen might admire lionlike courage, but they wouldn't care for such in their wives. No wonder her darling was crying out her eyes night after night. 'Twould do no good to beg the Major to stop Miss Samantha from going away.

Shaking her head, Bunch left the room, leaving Wyndham puzzled and obscurely hurt. Where was the girl, anyway?

The pale November sun was attempting unsuccessfully to combat the chill of a brisk north wind that whipped the skirts of Samantha's shabby brown pelisse. It was her last day at the Pillars, and she walked under the leafless branches of the lime trees, saying a poignant farewell to the gardens and walks she loved so well. Her trunk was packed, sitting corded and labeled in her bare room, waiting to be brought down tomorrow morning for the trip to London. There was nothing left to do but wait out these last, sad hours. Determined to go, having resisted Bunch's tears and Aunt Hester's staunch opposition, only one last doubt assailed her; whether to tell the Major good-bye in person or to allow the carefully worded note that Robert had been instructed to deliver tomorrow morning say it for her.

She longed to tell him how very grateful she was for all his kindnesses and beg his forgiveness for causing so much trouble and pain. But was it wise? Despite all her good intentions, she might embarrass them both with a spill of tears.

She had misjudged him, thought him cold and unfeeling when he was but wisely restrained. Priding herself on her sympathy for Huddle and the others, she now had to admit that the Major had given more help to the tenants in a few short weeks than she had been able to achieve in all her years of effort on their behalf.

Even Jasper was singing his praises. He had returned from an interview with Major Crawford actually glowing. The Major had thanked him for his courage at the quarry and offered him the loan for his stud farm in Ireland. A smile lit up Samantha's face at the recollection of Jasper's happiness.

"Oh, Sam," he exclaimed, "it's like a miracle!" Then drawing her into the morning room, he had, with a touching show of embarrassment, asked her again if she would do him the honor of becoming his wife. "I can afford to set up a house now, and oddly enough it don't seem such a bad idea."

"It's not a bad idea at all . . . but not with me."

"We'll be comfortable, Sam," he promised handsomely. "And it's a lot better for you than being a companion to some old crone."

"Thank you, Jasper, but no. It wouldn't do for either of us."

No amount of persuasion on Jasper's part could sway Samantha, but when he finally took his leave, he had wrung a promise from her that if she ever needed any help, she was to come to him.

Samantha appreciated his concern but hoped she'd never have cause to turn to him. The role she had chosen for herself might be hard, but new scenes and new acquaintances would also be a welcome relief from the painful thoughts that beset her. When she remembered how she had tried to hate Wyndham Crawford for judging her so unfairly, Samantha was tormented by the cruelest of regrets. Now knowing the truth, she realized that he had reason for his distrust, dislike even. Not once since that night had he asked to see her.

Her wandering feet had brought her near the house again, but she turned into the rose garden where an arbor of hanging briers sheltered a small love scat. Sitting dolefully on the rusty bench, Samantha was too lost in thought to heed approaching footsteps.

CHAPTER 20

A firm tread crushed the brittle, fallen leaves that were scattered on the path. Major Crawford had given up waiting and, despite nurse Bunch's dour predictions of disaster, had dressed himself and gone in search of Samantha.

He expected to find her in the morning room at this hour, but when a brief look disclosed the absence of even her embroidery frame, he rang for Jenny and asked roughly where her mistress could be found. Wyndham had begun to fear that Hester's news had come too late. Had the silly chit left the Pillars already? Lady Fitz had been too distraught to make much sense when she entered his room and besought him to reason with Samantha.

"I am at my wit's end," she wailed, putting a lace-trimmed hankie to her reddened eyes. "She is going away, and nothing I say will dissuade her. It's all Jasper's fault."

Wyndham's initial reaction was stunned disbelief, but Hester soon convinced him that this was not just another of her grand fusses. It appeared that Miss Crawford was leaving the Pillars—forever.

Could she have gone without telling me, Wyndham wondered as he glared at the little maid?

"Please, sir. She's in the garden."

"In this weather?" he growled testily. His sense of ill usage was increasing with every passing moment and by the time his pursuit of Samantha led out of doors, he was fighting a very real sense of injustice. How selfish and inconsiderate she was to upset her great-aunt in this way. If she wanted to marry Jasper, she at least could go through the proper motions. There was no need to run off from her family without a word. He would see that she was married properly and with all due ceremony, whether she liked it or not.

Too proud to take anything from me, he grumbled. But Samantha's stubborn pride was not the crux of the problem, and he knew it. It was the fact that she clearly intended to leave without a word to him that rankled. To beg her to stay as he longed to would be merely futile. She was in love with her silly, charming cousin and evidently more than ready to run away with him in a most unorthodox fashion.

Yet under all the surface bluster, Wyndham had a real fear that perhaps Samantha's steady refusal to see him all week had a deeper cause than just excitement at her impending nuptials. That ill-fated kiss! Little wonder that she avoided him like the plague. But when he lay wounded in the tunnel, Samantha had been caring, even tender. Wyndham had dared hope that she had finally forgiven him. But for what? The kiss, or his wild charge that she was concealing information? He had made a complete fool of himself

243

on both counts. No wonder the girl didn't want to speak to him. Never mind. He'd force her if necessary. If she could be kind to him when she thought he was dying, she could at least be civil now that he was alive and well.

Major Crawford had not yet decided what he was going to say to Samantha when he spied her in the rose garden. She didn't look like a happy bride on the eve of her wedding, but rather as if the biting wind had robbed her of all vitality. And why had she pulled her hair back so severely in that spinsterish way again? Feeling sad, was she, he thought grimly? And so she should. That Dakins lad would lead her a merry dance.

Samantha heard someone enter the arbor, but thinking it was only Bunch come to coax her in, she kept her tear-stained face averted. A stern voice brought her head swiftly around.

"I hear you are leaving us, Miss Crawford," the Major remarked coldly.

The surprise of finding the Major frowning down at her rendered Samantha momentarily speechless, but she recovered herself sufficiently to answer. "I leave in the morning."

"Without a word to me," he affirmed, his lips thinned in disapproval.

"I know what you think of the move I'm making, but I see no need to discuss it further. Why should we quarrel? I am of age, and my decision was made long ago." He was angry with her and little wonder, she thought. She'd given him nought but trouble. "I owe you an apology for my rash behavior the night

244

of the . . . the night you were wounded. I'm dreadfully sorry. You had everything in hand, and my attempts to help Jasper and the tenants were simply useless . . . and dangerous."

Wyndham gazed at her in surprise, not liking this newfound humility. "You weren't to know that."

"Nevertheless, you almost died because of my ill-planned heroics."

"Because of Parr, you mean. If he hadn't found an opportunity that night, another would have suited him as well." So she blamed herself. Poor Samantha. That must be a bitter pill for her to swallow, he thought, her woebegone face beginning to stir his heart. "I have cause to thank you, Miss Crawford. Lieutenant Travers tells me that without your care, I would have bled to death on the ride home."

"Nonsense. Anyone could have done the same. But should you be standing here? The wind is too chill; you are not well. I wonder that Bunch has allowed you out."

"My good woman, I am not a child to be bullied by the dictates of a nurse."

"Of course not, Major," Samantha answered docilely.

"And you can take that know-it-all look off your face."

"Do not provoke me, Major Crawford. I have vowed never to lose my temper again, but you are trying my endurance."

"Good. I never did like that whey-faced creature you pretended to be."

"Pretended! I was a model of decorum before I met you."

"And damned dull to boot."

"Thank you," Samantha said coldly. "I will always treasure that compliment."

The Major sat down next to her and gave a weary sigh. "I warned you I'm no hand with words. All I do is set your back up every time I try to make amends. I'm so used to bellowing, it's become a habit."

"Yes, I'd noticed. But I'm beginning to get accustomed to it."

"Then you've forgiven me?"

"Major Crawford," Samantha answered with heartfelt sincerity, "I am the one who craves forgiveness. You not only proved me wrong, but saved everyone in the process. And your generosity to Jasper exceeds all bounds."

"He saved my life. And so did you."

"Jasper told me how he came to warn you, and how you managed to turn that warning into a plan to save everyone. It would be more correct to say that you saved his life. For that I will be endlessly grateful." She turned to the Major spontaneously. "He can be a terrible fool, but he is my cousin, you understand."

"I see you are awake on every suit." Wyndham was exasperated. If Samantha knew her cousin's character so well, why in heaven's name did she want to marry him? The thought was becoming increasingly intolerable. "Would you think ill of me if I asked you to change your plans?" he said baldly.

"It would be like you," Samantha answered. How very kind of the Major to still want to offer her a home at the Pillars after all this unpleasantness. But, of course, it was out of the question. She'd never manage to keep up this show of friendly disinterest seeing him day after day.

Wyndham was baffled and very far from pleased by what he considered her strange reply. Was it like him to lure away another man's bride? The fact that he was trying to do that very thing had no bearing on the case, he argued silently to himself.

"But I couldn't stay here." Samantha continued guilelessly, having no idea how she was confusing the poor man as he labored to make sense of their conversation.

"Is it still taking my charity that galls you?" Wyndham asked impatiently.

"That's not the problem, Major."

"Then stay here where you are appreciated."

"I'll be appreciated more where I'm going."

The Major lost his temper again. "But why such a rush? Do you and Dakins have to run off together? I'll pay for a wedding if you're so eager to marry him. But I tell you now, you are making the mistake of your life. How long do you think you'll be satisfied playing mother hen to him? He's no match for you. Besides, it's my money that's setting him up, after all. You needn't marry him to get it. I've been offering it for weeks with no strings attached."

Samantha was regarding him in total bewilderment until his last words brought an angry flush to her cheeks. "I wouldn't touch one penny of your precious money. Even marrying Jasper is preferable to that, although I can't imagine where you got the harebrained notion. I am marrying no one."

The Major gave an enraged bellow. "Then where in God's name are you running off to?"

"I do not appreciate profanity, Major," Samantha said calmly, "but you know quite well I'm off to London to be a companion to Mrs. Featherstone-Hornby."

In answer to that, the Major enveloped Samantha in a bear hug and roared in her ear, "You are the most pigheaded woman I've ever known. Surrender your stupid pride and stay here."

Samantha struggled to free herself. "Let me go. I've told you, I will not be bullied by you."

Wyndham loosened his hold and said in an odd voice, "Is it my scar? I'll understand if it's too much to think of seeing every day."

"Confound your scar! It's the most human thing about you. Now will you let me go?"

"Not until you agree to marry me."

There was a note of uncertainty in his voice that was completely new, and Samantha raised her eyes sharply up to him to see if he could be bamming her. "Did Aunt Hester put you up to this?"

That charge did the Major's already turbulent emotions no good at all. "Devil take you, woman! I don't jump to petticoat orders." At which point he lost all patience and kissed her soundly.

This time Samantha felt no urge to strike him. She did think that her dignity was somewhat endangered by the madly fluttering action of her heart, but the Major seemed to be in no better state than she was.

"I don't understand," was all she could say when Wyndham finally released her.

"I thought it was obvious. My heart has been hanging out my sleeve ever since I first saw you."

"Never, Major. You disliked me intensely."

"Blast you, Samantha. Are we going to argue over my proposal of marriage?"

"Proposal? You ordered me to marry you."

"So you will then," he said and held her tighter.

Samantha made no immediate protest, but did arch slightly back so she could see his face. "Is this how you took Salamanca, by brute force?"

"With cannons blazing. I'm a cavalry man, don't forget."

"As if I could. Then why don't you open fire?"

The Major smiled at the command in her voice and responded to her call to arms with a direct frontal attack. He stormed the citadel and laid siege to his captive, who offered no resistance. In fact she surrendered immediately. Victory was his without even a battle.

THE DARK HORSEMAN

Marianne Harvey
author of *The Proud Hunter*

Beautiful Donna Penroze had sworn to her dying father that she would save her sole legacy, the crumbling tin mines and the ancient, desolate estate *Trencobban*. But the mines were failing, and Donna had no one to turn to. No one except the mysterious Nicholas Trevarvas—rich, arrogant, commanding. Donna would do anything but surrender her pride, anything but admit her irresistible longing for *The Dark Horseman*.

A Dell Book $3.25